Looking for a silver lining

"If you do a report on the vice principal, you're almost guaranteed an easy A. Do you think the teacher is going to take a chance on putting a lower grade on the paper about her boss?"

Sabrina thought about that for a moment. "Okay, so there is something potentially okay about doing that report."

Josh helped her put the dirty dishes in the dishwasher trays and throw the rest of the refuse away. "You just have to look for the silver lining in the dark clouds, Sabrina."

"You know, I think maybe you're right." But she knew she was getting totally desperate if Mr. Kraft was her silver lining. *Things can't get any lower, can they?*

Titles in SABRINA, THE TEENAGE WITCH™
Pocket Books series:

All Pocket Book titles are available by post from:
Sumon & Schuster Cash Sales, P.O. Box 29, Douglas, Isle of Man IM99 1BQ
Credit cards accepted. Please telephone 01624 836000,
Fax 01624 670923, Internet http://www.bookpost.co.uk
or email: bookshop@enterprise.net for details

Mummy Dearest

Mel Odom

Based upon the characters in Archie Comics

And based upon the television series
Sabrina, The Teenage Witch
Created for television by Nell Scovell
Developed for television by Jonathan Schmock

POCKET
BOOKS

LONDON · SYDNEY · NEW YORK

POCKET
B O O K S

An imprint of Simon & Schuster UK Ltd
Africa House, 64-78 Kingsway
London WC2B 6AH

ISBN 0 671 77324 0

1 3 5 7 9 10 8 6 4 2

Printed by Omnia Books Ltd, Glasgow

This book is dedicated to Stacy DeFoe, Julie Asbury, Jennifer Crotteau, Sara Wilson, Christy Curtis, Jill Hinckley, Brooke Raymond, Michelle Trujillo, and Andrea Banse, who keep computer and console gaming in the fast lane.

Mummy Dearest

Chapter 1

Sabrina Spellman stood in front of the full-length mirror in her bedroom and pointed up outfit after outfit. Since she was a witch, she could change her look in the blink of an eye, from clothing to makeup to hairstyle. She whirled before the mirror, catching herself in different poses and with different expressions.

No, she thought, pointing her finger at her image and erasing the spring green women's suit she'd been modeling in the mirror. Instantly she was dressed in a light blue skirt with little yellow baby ducks on it and a white blouse with frilly sleeves.

She looked at herself in the mirror and tried different poses. The oh-wow-look-at-me-be-surprised look didn't quite come together. The I'm-so-calm-

I'm-to-die-for look appeared contrived. And even the innocent look crumpled.

"This is not as easy as it looks," she grumbled in frustration. She pointed the spring garments away and tried a beach look with khaki pants rolled to mid-calf and a lemon-yellow midi-blouse that left her stomach and shoulders bare.

In the mirror she didn't look beachy at all. She looked more like a girl standing in front of her mirror with rolled-up pants and pale skin. If she was going to look as if she was out for a stroll along the beach, she needed a tan.

Pointing again, she applied a tan that left her golden-bronze. *Oh, yeah, now that's better. Maybe something a little more daring, though.* She pointed again. Instantly magical sparkles shot from her finger and swirled over her left cheek. A rainbow-colored butterfly tattoo popped into place on her cheek.

Sabrina grinned at her reflection. *Now, that was different. If her aunts could only see her now, they'd—*

"Sabrina Spellman!"

Ooops! Looking in the mirror, Sabrina spotted Aunt Hilda standing in the door of her room.

"What have you done to your face?" Hilda stepped into the room and took Sabrina's chin in her hand, turning her head to the side so she could get a better look.

"It's a butterfly," Sabrina explained.

"No," Hilda said firmly, "it's gone." She pointed. Sabrina felt a small tingle on her cheek, then felt

2

the harsh scrub of a washcloth applied none too gently. "Ow, ow ow ow!" She grabbed Hilda's hands and stepped back. "That hurts."

"Good," Hilda said. "Do you know what your father would have said if he'd seen you with a tattoo?"

"He wouldn't have seen me."

Hilda arched her brows. "Do you think he wouldn't have noticed something like that?"

"No, what I meant was this is just homework."

"Homework?" Hilda looked doubtful.

"The Career Day paper," Sabrina reminded. "You remember. Mrs. Paxton told our class she was going to assign a paper we were supposed to write about a career." Career Day was on Wednesday next week. Sabrina and Harvey had been busy making decorations and notices all week to hang out in the hall.

"And when did tattooing get to be a career? Not that it's ever going to be one in this household."

"Not tattooing. I'm going to do a paper on the career of a fashion photographer."

"What do you know about fashion photography?"

Sabrina sighed and regarded her image in the mirror. "Not as much as I'd hoped," she admitted. "In addition to the paper, Mrs. Paxton wants us to put together a portfolio of that career. I thought maybe I could take a few pictures of myself, but this isn't working out at all."

"Ahem."

Sabrina and Hilda glanced down at the floor. Salem, the Spellman family's black American shorthair cat, sat in the doorway. He wore a dark purple beret and a small camera around his neck.

"Perhaps I could offer my services," the cat said. He hadn't always been a cat. Once he'd been a warlock named Salem Saberhagen, but he'd tried to take over the world. As punishment, the Witches' Council had turned him into a cat for a hundred years and given him to Sabrina's aunts.

"What services?" Sabrina asked.

The cat blinked at her. "Why, as a photographer, of course. The way I see it, you're struggling to be a model and a photographer." He shook his head back and forth. "There's no way you can wear both hats."

"You've been a fashion photographer?" Much as she was inclined to disbelieve him, Salem *had* been a lot of things in his life. Besides an up-and-coming world conqueror and a cat.

"But of course." Salem turned a paw up daintily and sniffed. "I worked with all the big ones."

"Who?" Hilda demanded.

Salem slitted his eyes. "I'm not in the habit of dropping names. *Très gauche.*"

"And here I thought *gauche* was a way of life for you."

"You've never paid attention to my finer qualities." Salem shifted his gaze to Sabrina. "Remember, I was considered a very talented *artiste* for a while."

That's true, Sabrina had to admit. Unfortunately, Salem's meteoric career as an artist had lasted only a very brief time.

"You got lucky," Hilda grumped.

4

"I would say that was a catty remark," Salem responded, "but I generally only reserve that designation for very wise statements that come from the mouths of cats. Mainly me."

Sabrina was torn. The paper was due on Monday, and so far she'd only done a little research because she'd been concentrating on getting the photographer's portfolio together. After all, a teacher would rather look at pictures, right?

A burning smell filled the air.

"What's on fire?" Sabrina asked.

"Breakfast." Hilda frowned. "I thought we'd have something more than Happy-Os for breakfast today." She glanced at Sabrina. "Since I thought you were up early enough to eat."

"What were we having?" Sabrina crinkled her nose against the smell.

"Belgian waffles."

"Hey," Salem said. "I could go for a Belgian waffle." He licked his chops. "Um, hot waffle drowned in maple syrup, filled with tiny anchovy bits and sprinkled with catnip." He sighed.

Hilda gave him a look of disgust. "There goes my appetite. For maybe a week."

"Actually," Sabrina said, thinking she'd like to give Salem a chance at being a photographer without her aunt knowing, "Belgian waffles sounds great. Is any there chance of a salvage mission?"

"I'll go check," Hilda said, "but I've smelled that degree of burn before. I think it was the Great

Chicago Fire of 1871, or maybe a California forest fire." She popped out of the room.

Sabrina looked at Salem. "Do you really think you can do this?"

The cat used a French accent. "But of course! Poof! You are in the hands of a master, *chérie!*"

"Actually, I don't have anything to lose." Sabrina had considered asking Harvey to photograph her, but that hadn't been appealing because she didn't want him to think she was stuck on herself. Although some of the outfits she'd whipped up had looked truly awesome.

"Then we are a match." Salem waited, bumping the tip of his tail against the floor patiently.

"Do you like this outfit?" Sabrina gestured at the beach ensemble.

"I can work with it." Salem still wasn't moving.

"We don't have all morning," Sabrina said.

"We haven't discussed my fee."

"Your fee?"

"Artists don't work for free," Salem stated.

"I thought artists did it for the enjoyment of practicing their craft."

"Not this artist."

Sabrina sighed. "There's nothing worse than a greedy cat. Are we talking belly rub here or massive ear scratching?"

"We're talking about a favor to be named later."

"No way."

"Fine. *Au revoir, chérie.*" Salem flicked his beret forward with a paw and turned to go.

"Wait. A favor to be named later." Sabrina thought desperately. She had a good grade in business class, but Mrs. Paxton was weighting the Career Day paper so it counted a lot. "How bad could it be? Right?"

Salem smiled. "Exactly. So do we go to work, or am I off to breakfast?"

Checking the clock, Sabrina saw that she had a few minutes left. "Work."

"Favor?"

Sabrina decided to play hard. "It depends on how the pictures turn out. If they're as good as you say they will be, fine. But if they're not, no favors."

The cat's smile stayed in place, but Sabrina thought there was a little more effort this time. "Pressure makes it harder for an artist to work."

"I could always go to the mall," Sabrina countered.

"They'd charge you an arm and a leg," Salem objected.

"At least I'd know what it was costing me up front."

Hilda suddenly reappeared in the room. "The Belgian waffles I was making are officially toast, so I'm off to Belgium to get breakfast. I'll be back in ten minutes. Be ready." She disappeared again.

Sabrina glanced at Salem. "Think of it as an audition."

"Fine," Salem grumbled. He padded into the room and leaped onto the bed. "Get ready to turn on that charisma. I wish we had a decent studio."

Even though it was only Salem and she didn't really believe he could do what he said he could, Sabrina felt a little nervous. Everyone in the class was going to review each other's assignments, getting information about a lot of different careers.

Salem put the camera on the bed, then lay behind it so he could peer through the viewfinder. He rolled his paw over the lens to adjust it.

At least he seems to know what he's doing, Sabrina thought.

"Okay, give me the beach look," Salem coaxed.

Sabrina smiled one of her best smiles.

"More beach," Salem directed, snapping off picture after picture. "I need to feel the wind and smell the sea. Give me some movement. I need sand, Sabrina, give me sand."

Sabrina tried following Salem's directions but ended up getting confused.

"Give me attitude," Salem said, taking another picture.

Turning her head, Sabrina tried to project confidence.

"Not confidence," Salem told her. "Attitude, attitude. Give me something that will just dare people to come up to get to know you. Defiance. Unapproachability."

Sabrina tried but didn't feel comfortable. "Unapproachable? That's not me. I'm Miss Congeniality." She grinned a big grin. "See?"

Salem glanced from behind the camera. He glared in frustration. "You're hard to work with."

"Well," Sabrina said, putting her hands on her hips, "maybe I'm better at this than I thought. Get your camera ready because we're moving on from unapproachable to difficult."

"Okay." Salem sighed. The flash burst a few more times. "Difficult, then. I can work with that. But give me difficult with a hat."

Sabrina pointed up a white beach hat and flipped the brim up. She started moving around the room, trying not to feel too goofy.

"Give me another hat," Salem directed, rolling over the bed with the camera between his paws, shooting shot after shot. "A baseball cap. A pony-tail. Wraparound sunglasses."

Sabrina pointed everything into place.

"Oh, yeah," Salem enthused, shooting pictures. "Now you're getting it. That's it. Work it, work it. Let it all hang out. You're beautiful, baby, just beautiful."

Suddenly suspicious, Sabrina stopped looking as though she were peering out to sea. "Salem."

"What?" The cat rolled on the bed, still clicking the shutter. "Don't stop now. This stuff is pure gold. Trust me."

"How many pictures are on that roll of film?" Sabrina asked.

Salem stopped clicking the camera shutter. "Film?" He glanced at the camera. "How about that? I could have sworn there was film in the camera." He slipped a paw behind his beret and scratched.

"Sabrina," Hilda called from downstairs.

"Coming," Sabrina replied. She made a face at the cat. "Some *artiste*." She pointed a new outfit for

9

herself, a royal blue midi-dress, and styled her hair, letting it hang down to her shoulders. Her finger felt a little strained from the morning's activity.

"Hey, if I'd had film in the camera, you'd have thought I was a genius."

"Well, at least you're safe from that." Sabrina grabbed her bookbag and headed downstairs. Both her aunts were in the kitchen when she arrived there. The toasty sweet smell of Belgian waffles and hot maple syrup filled the room.

Hilda set the table with a single point, then took a seat.

Aunt Zelda sat at one end of the breakfast bar, toying with the pieces of an antique radio spread out on the counter before her. Blond and vivacious, Zelda was chronically working on one thing or another, usually in the field of quantum mechanics.

"Don't tell me," Sabrina said, taking a seat at the table. "You're putting a radio together for someone who couldn't fix it."

"No." Zelda moved a tiny piece into place with a pair of tweezers. "I'm attempting to repair and restore a family heirloom that was recently recovered from the attic."

Sabrina took a waffle and smothered it in butter and syrup. "Why don't you just point it back together?"

Zelda glanced at her over the half-glasses she wore. "Because you have to be careful about pointing antiquities back together. Sometimes a little magic can rub off on them, enchant them, and create problems."

"That whole Arabian lamp thing got way beyond control," Hilda agreed. "But things worked out in the end. With a little nudge along the way."

"Aladdin's lamp?" Sabrina asked.

"That's the one." Zelda pushed the pieces around on the countertop and frowned. "These little gears are starting to look all the same."

"Waffle?" Hilda offered. "Fresh from Belgium this morning. I've even got real cream and strawberries for the educated palate." Her waffle was piled over with the bright red berries and white cream.

"Like there's something wrong with syrup."

"Not really wrong." Salem hopped up onto the breakfast bar and eyed the clock pieces with bright interest. "It just lacks a little verve."

"Touch those pieces," Zelda warned, "and your next trip outside this house will be to the taxidermist."

Salem retreated from the clock pieces. "One phone call to the SPCA and you won't threaten me like that."

"No threat. It's a promise." Zelda looked at the stack of waffles. "One of those and I'll be on the exercise bike an extra hour this week."

Hilda took a bite and looked totally blissful. "You've been dating long enough that an extra pound or two shouldn't come between you and darling Willard."

Ugh! Sabrina's stomach revolted. She still couldn't believe that her aunt was dating Mr. Kraft, the vice principal.

"You're probably right." Zelda joined them at the table. "But I'll just have one."

"Hey, what about the cat?" Salem asked. "How come nobody feeds the cat? I've got paws. Have you ever tried to use a can opener with paws?"

"No," Hilda said. "But, then, I've never been turned into a cat for a lifetime, either."

"A few other utterly disgusting things," Zelda agreed. "But never a cat."

Before her aunts could start one of their familiar bickering sessions over Willard Kraft and Zelda's attraction for him, Sabrina said, "So how are things at the shop?" She pointed a waffle over to Salem.

"How about a little tuna preserves to top it off?" the cat asked.

Sabrina added the tuna with a point and tried to control her purge reflex. Sometimes she wondered what Salem's tastes would be like once he became a warlock again.

"Things are picking up," Zelda said cautiously, spooning strawberries over her waffle.

"Translation," Salem said. "They've still got a lot of time on their hands." He cracked up at his own joke, waving his paw in the air.

Hilda pointed at the cat's waffle, and the tuna preserves evaporated.

"Nooooo!" Salem squawked. "That's not fair!" He started sobbing.

Zelda ignored the feline. "How's the Career Day report coming?"

"It's okay." Sabrina braced herself, knowing if Zelda was inquiring about how a project was going it was because her aunt had a hidden agenda.

"How much information have you gathered on fashion photography?"

"Enough," Sabrina answered.

"I thought maybe you were having problems finishing your report, so I was going to suggest an alternative career to write about."

"No, really," Sabrina replied. "The fashion photography piece is working out."

"Someone else might be doing a similar report," Zelda persisted.

"Mrs. Paxton said that would be okay." Sabrina tried to keep up the conversation, eat the waffle quickly, and not choke while doing them both. "She expects a certain amount of repetition."

"The star group," Hilda said. "Sports star, music star, movie star."

"Right." Sabrina rushed her last bite of waffle and hurried her plate to the dishwasher.

"I was just thinking you might prefer something different," Zelda said. "Did you know the Swiss clock industry is still thriving? And a number of them are using skills handed down through the families."

"Uh, I'll look into it if the fashion photography falls through." Sabrina looked at her watch. "Wow, can you believe the time." She grabbed her backpack and headed for the door. "Gotta go."

Outside, she leaned into her walk because she really was cutting the time close. Luckily, the trip to Westbridge High was a short one and the weather was good. She hurried through the halls, looking for Harvey, hoping to get in a brief conversation before the class bell rang.

"Miss Spellman."

Sabrina recognized Mr. Kraft's voice even over the conversational buzz that filled the hallway. "Uh-oh." She slowed immediately, then turned. That tone of voice always meant trouble.

☆

Chapter 2

Mr. Kraft stood at the other end of the hallway, his arms folded across his chest. He wasn't smiling, but then he never really smiled except when he was with Aunt Zelda. However, he wasn't frowning that frown that usually meant bad news.

Sabrina walked back toward him. "I wasn't running through the halls. Really. I can understand how it might have looked that way because I was kind of in a hurry. And maybe my knees were a little high, but the aerobics tape I've been working out to emphasizes high knee movement." *The last thing I need right now is detention. That would crowd out what little social life I'm going to get before I go to work at the coffee shop.*

"Don't worry about that." Mr. Kraft waved the possibility away. Then he smiled. The vice principal's smile was enough to send most students into catatonic shock. "I've got another matter in mind I'd like to discuss with you." He smiled again.

Bad news, Sabrina thought furiously, *bad news, gotta be bad news.* But she smiled and said, "Sure." Her smile didn't stay. "What?"

Mr. Kraft pushed his glasses up. "I wanted to talk to you about the Career Day paper you're writing."

"Aunt Zelda told you about it?" *Ewwww.* Having Mr. Kraft dating Zelda was bad enough, but she couldn't let him prowl around in Sabrina's life. That was so—so *uncool!*

"No," Mr. Kraft said. "I haven't talked to her about it. Although maybe I should have because you'd have been better prepared for the changes Mrs. Paxton has made in the assignment."

"What changes?" Now there was potential unhappiness.

"Mrs. Paxton decided that Career Day might be better represented if the students did a paper on one of their parents' careers instead of whatever they wanted."

"Parents?" Sabrina could not believe it. *Who would want to write about their parents?*

"It doesn't really have to be about their parents." Mr. Kraft waved her over to the side of the hall away from the other students. "I checked."

"That's good."

"Actually, it can be about anyone in the family." Mr. Kraft looked embarrassed as he went on. "Or it can even be about anyone who's on the *verge* of becoming part of the family."

Sabrina experienced a sudden sinking in her stomach. "Maybe I should wait until Mrs. Paxton tells me about the changes."

"You don't have to." Mr. Kraft waved a warning finger at a trio of boys goofing off with each other down the hall. They straightened up immediately. Normally that was a detention offense. "I already did." The vice principal rubbed his hands together briskly. "Zelda and I talked about your project the other night. She didn't tell me about it. I just—well, I just kind of asked. I know how you work really hard for your grades and I wanted you to have every opportunity. I know you don't have much contact with your parents, so I thought the assignment might be a little more difficult for you than some of the kids."

"Oh." *That's diplomatic, isn't it?*

"I just wanted you to know that there were some alternatives," Mr. Kraft said.

"Aunt Zelda mentioned watch-making as a potential career subject."

Mr. Kraft looked surprised. "She did?"

"Yes."

The vice principal shook his head. "She didn't know about the changes. Of course, you could do a paper on your aunt's work in the area of quantum mechanics, but I thought that could be a little ambitious."

Harvey Kinkle, her boyfriend, walked by with a couple of his friends. He wore a green and white baseball jersey over a green T-shirt and jeans, looking totally cute. He frowned sympathetically at Sabrina, gave her a small wave, and kept going.

Sabrina didn't blame him for not stopping long enough to say hi. "Quantum mechanics wouldn't be a first choice for me."

"That's what I thought," Mr. Kraft said. "I was also thinking you might want to do your report on a career with real challenge and human interest."

"A career like what?" Sabrina couldn't believe she'd actually asked, knowing where the conversation had to be leading.

"Like the career of a high school vice principal." Mr. Kraft looked at her expectantly.

Not trusting herself to say anything, Sabrina remained quiet. She tried to remember if she'd broken any bad-luck taboos. If this were a bad-luck witch day of any kind, her aunts would have mentioned it.

"I okayed it with Mrs. Paxton," Mr. Kraft said. "If you want, you can start today."

"Today?"

Mr. Kraft nodded. "Sure. Observing me. Following me around. Asking me questions about the things I do."

Luckily, the first bell rang then. The students in the halls scattered, moving toward their homerooms under the vigilant gaze of the vice principal. Mr. Kraft held his pen and paper poised, ready to write down any slackers.

"Maybe I should check with Mrs. Paxton." Sabrina eased off and tried to go down the hall.

"Aren't you interested in doing your paper on me?" Mr. Kraft asked.

It's not quite as bad as an incurable illness, Sabrina told herself. But she had to tell him the truth, didn't she? She stopped herself just in time. "Mr. Kraft, I think that assignment would be too ambitious. Covering quantum mechanics has got to be a lot easier. I mean, just think about all the drama, human emotion, and torture—uh, tenure."

"You could do it," Mr. Kraft said. "I have faith in you. After all, you'll have me as a living, breathing reference."

Panicking, Sabrina pointed toward the school bell on the wall high on the opposite wall. Her magic caused it to ring immediately, catching some of the students out in the hall.

Mr. Kraft jumped toward them at once. "You, you, you, and you," he said in a loud voice as he wrote furiously on the pad. "All of you are late to class. Come get your detention slips."

A dozen kids came over to the vice principal with glum faces.

"Mr. Kraft," Sabrina said, pointing at the clock. "According to the time, they still have a minute to get to class. Something must be wrong with the bell." She didn't want anyone to have to go to detention because she was trying to escape the vice principal.

Mr. Kraft looked up at the clock and saw that time yet remained. "Okay," he told the group, "get to class. I'm letting you off easy this time."

The students wasted no time in blazing trails down the hall.

"And no running," Mr. Kraft thundered. He turned back to Sabrina. "I can free up this afternoon if you'd like. For you, I mean, so you can interview me for the paper."

"I appreciate that, Mr. Kraft," Sabrina said, "but I really don't think I could do the interview justice."

The vice principal looked at her blankly. "You don't?"

The final bell rang again, this time for real.

"No," Sabrina said.

"That's too bad." Mr. Kraft tried not to show his hurt feelings. He put the detention slips he'd written for the other students in his jacket pocket. Scribbling hurriedly, he tore off a slip and handed it to Sabrina. "You'll need an admit to class now that you're late. It was my fault for keeping you."

"Thank you."

Mr. Kraft wrote out another slip and handed it to her.

Sabrina took it and looked at DETENTION written heavily across the top. "Detention?"

"You were running in the halls," Mr. Kraft said. "You had high knees."

"I thought you told me not to worry about that."

Mr. Kraft nodded. "I did, I did. And if you were doing that interview, one of the things I'd instruct you in is the prerogative for a vice principal to change his mind. Have a good day, Sabrina, and I'll see you for detention this afternoon."

Stunned, Sabrina watched him walk away.

"I'd hurry along to class if I were you," Mr. Kraft called. "Without running. That hall pass has an expiration time on it."

Sabrina looked at the hall pass to find it did have an expiration time on it. She had less than a minute to get to class. She turned and hurried down the hall, double-time without running. Still, she was out of breath by the time she reached Mrs. Paxton's business class.

Mrs. Paxton stood at the front of the class in front of the dry-erase board. She was tall, dark-haired, and in her early twenties. She wore a business suit, bringing off the total professional look. The changes for the Career Day assignment were written in four different marker colors on the board behind her. *Parents* was underlined in each of those colors.

The students didn't look happy. Sabrina didn't blame them. She put her hall pass on Mrs. Paxton's desk and took her seat beside Harvey up front.

"Why do we have to write about our parents?" Marjorie Timmons asked. She was petite and blond, always trying to get into the in-group at school.

"I was talking to Mr. Kraft yesterday," Mrs. Paxton said.

The whole class groaned.

"And," the business teacher went on, "Mr. Kraft and I were talking about how much more productive Career Day could be if we could have at least one parent from each student show up to give a brief talk about what they do. However, that's really impossible because so many parents can't spare the time to come. I can't remember who, but Mr. Kraft or I thought it would be a good idea if each student wrote about one parent instead."

"When will the paper be due?" Harvey asked.

"On Monday."

The class groaned again.

"But," Mrs. Paxton said, "that's not as bad as it sounds. I'm not going to expect as much in-depth information as we'd previously discussed. I just want to know a little about one of your parents and what they do."

"Yes," asked a student, "but which parent?"

"I'm leaving that up to you."

"Oh."

Sabrina was bummed. Due to her special nature as a witch, she wasn't able to see her mother for two years or her mom would be turned into a ball of wax. Most of that two years was up now, but there was no way she could interview her. Even if the Witches' Council did allow any other kind of contact like the phone or e-mail, her mom wasn't always near telecommunications, or electricity, for that matter. She was always off in remote places doing archeological research.

"You can do two papers if you wish," Mrs. Paxton said. "That way you don't have to choose."

"You're going to be reading a lot of boring papers," said another student, Helen Wu, with a smile. New in class, she was here temporarily because her mother had some glamorous diplomatic job and had to travel all over the world.

"I'm sure yours won't be, Helen." Mrs. Paxton smiled.

A shy smile formed on Helen's face. "I had been working on another career choice," she said. "Fashion photography. I'd—I'd like to show you the portfolio I've put together." She took a thick expand-a-file from her book bag and placed it on her desk.

"I'd love to see it," Mrs. Paxton said. "Now, if there aren't any more questions, we'll move on to today's assignment."

Totally bummed, Sabrina took her book from her bag and opened it on her desk. How could anyone be cruel enough to assign a student a paper about their parents? What could anyone possibly want to know about their parents? Outside of uphill-through-the-snow-both-ways-to-school, what was there to learn?

She glanced at the thick folder on Helen's desk. But maybe it was a blessing. Poses by Salem were never going to compete with that.

Of course, there was always Mr. Kraft's offer, and accepting it would get her out of detention. *That's about as attractive as sprouting a new head to get a new look. Give me detention.*

Chapter 3

☆

"What did Mr. Kraft bust you for in the hall this morning, Sab?"

"He wanted me to do his life story." Sabrina went to her locker with Harvey in tow. "I wasn't interested, so he gave me detention for running in the hall."

"What?"

"I know. I can't believe it, either." Sabrina put her business book and bookbag away, and took out the book she needed for her next class. "Since he and Mrs. Paxton talked, he found out that the *parent* could be another person of your family. Even someone who's about to become part of your family."

Harvey wrinkled his nose in disgust. "Mr. Kraft asked your aunt to marry him?"

"No, but even if he did, the really icky part would

24

be if she said yes." Sabrina shuddered, then closed her locker. "We're going to stop right there with that topic." She walked out into the hallway and joined the main flow of traffic.

"Sure. But I kind of like the idea that you could do the Career Day paper on someone else in the family."

"You don't want to do a paper on your parents?"

Harvey shrugged. "My mom stays at home and my dad's a pest-control tech."

"Kind of leaves you with the bugs, huh?"

"Yeah. And I don't really want to go there with my report. You know, talking about the kinds of places my dad goes into, the stuff that he sees. That *I* see." Harvey sometimes helped his dad out on big bug jobs. Unconsciously, he started scratching furiously at his neck and brushing at his hair. He caught himself and looked at Sabrina apologetically. "Sorry. Habit."

"Rudy Gellar would like to hear stories about bugs," Sabrina teased.

"Oh, man." Harvey shook his head. "I don't want to even be around anything Rudy Gellar is interested in. Did you hear that they banned him from the biology lab?"

"Yeah," Sabrina said, remembering. "I think the thing with the ketchup was the last straw."

"I couldn't go to the cafeteria for a week after that."

"Okay, if you don't do a report on your mom or dad, who would you do it on?"

"Uncle Herman," Harvey replied, smiling. "It'd be a great story. The Mafia contracted him to kill a guy."

"You're kidding." Sabrina racked her brain, trying to remember if Harvey had ever mentioned this uncle before. "Your uncle was a hit man for the Mob?" Her voice caught the attention of a few students around them.

Harvey threw an arm around her shoulders and hustled her through the suddenly interested group. He spoke in a lower voice. "No. He's a pest-control guy in New York. The Mafia guys that got in touch with him looked him up under Exterminators and didn't pay attention to who they were actually calling. They didn't tell Uncle Herman much about what he was getting contracted for, except that it was a big extermination."

"It was a guy."

"Yeah. Some guy turning state's evidence or something. They wanted him killed."

"So what did your uncle do when he found out what he was really being hired for?"

"It was Uncle Herman." Harvey shrugged. "He went to the police, agreed to wear a wire, and helped convict them. He helped put them in prison."

"Wow, so your uncle is a hero."

"I guess. He's in the Witness Protection Program somewhere. The Mafia guys took out a contract on him from some real hit men. They got connected in prison with some guys who knew some guys. Now, we get a card every so often from Uncle Herman." Harvey shook his head. "Of course, he's not Uncle Herman anymore. He's somebody else, but he just can't tell us who he is."

"Then how do you know the cards are from him?"

Confusion darkened Harvey's face. "You know, I guess we don't. Those cards could be from the hit men trying to get to Uncle Herman, thinking maybe we know something. I'm going to have to tell Dad about this." He left her at the door to her next class, forgetting even to tell her good-bye because he was so caught up in his new line of thinking.

"Bye, Harvey," Sabrina called. She turned and entered the class, still trying to figure out what she was going to do about the Career Day paper.

"You're home late today."

Sabrina glanced at Salem. The cat lay on the kitchen counter with a can of food unopened beside him. "Yes."

"Someone had a bad day."

"Someone," Sabrina said, "had detention."

Salem sat up and eyed her reproachfully. "We're going to have to talk about your attitude. If you have detention, the cat doesn't get his afternoon snack on time. See, since Hilda and Zelda went out shopping, they're not here for the afternoon snack feeding time."

Dropping her bookbag on the table, Sabrina picked up the can and used the electric opener. "You could have gone with them."

"I was going to, but . . ." Salem replied, watching the opening process with bright interest.

"They could have fed you at the mall." Sabrina emptied the can into the cat dish.

"If I'd gone." Salem stuck his muzzle in the cat dish and started munching.

Sudden realization hit Sabrina. She'd felt so aggravated about Mr. Kraft's unfair detention—well, for the most part it was unfair—that she hadn't been thinking. She glared at the cat suspiciously. "They fed you already, didn't they?"

Salem looked up at her, owl-eyed. "I don't know what you're talking about." His words came out muffled because his mouth was stuffed.

Sabrina pointed at her hand and the cordless phone appeared in it. "All it will take is one simple phone call," she threatened.

The cat broke down and started sobbing. "All right. I did it. I admit it. Hilda fed me my snack."

"So you just had to go and dump all this guilt on me?"

"I was hungry," Salem sobbed. "I couldn't help myself."

Exasperated, Sabrina pointed at the cat dish. Immediately the tender meaty chunks erupted from the bowl and smacked into Salem's face. "Cats." She turned and left the kitchen, taking the stairs up to her bedroom.

"Teenagers," the cat snarled back at her. "You know, throwing cat food around is all good fun until somebody loses an eye."

Sabrina pointed again, then listened to the satisfying smack of meaty chunks hitting the cat again.

"That's quite a mess you've left down here," Salem taunted. "In fact, I'd say it rates a—"

Halting at the top of the stairs, Sabrina pointed again and said,

Food that I opened when the cat meowed,
Can't be a mess. That's not allowed.

Immediately a fresh wave of sobbing came from the kitchen. "Noooo!" Salem sobbed. "Don't take it away!"

In her room Sabrina tossed her bookbag on her bed and pointed herself up some casual clothes. Depressed as she was, trapped with just a little while before she had to go to work and not having had her usual few minutes to spend with Harvey after school, she chose a sweatshirt and shorts so she could really feel sorry for herself. But she was only going to feel sorry for herself for a little while. She wasn't going to make a career of it.

And there was that word again: *career.* That was the real problem.

She sat on the bed and looked at the pictures she had of her mom and dad on the bureau. Her dad wore a black tuxedo and looked every inch the polished gentleman. The picture she had of her mom was on an archeological dig in South America. It was a candid shot, not posed at all, a favorite Sabrina had chosen from a packet her mom had sent.

Her mom had blond hair and a fair complexion as well. She was more tanned than Sabrina because of constant exposure to the sun and wind. She wore khaki shorts and a white sleeveless blouse, and her pith helmet was tilted back. Dirt stained her mom's garments and face as she brushed at the pottery bowl she held. Excitement and awe filled her face.

"Mind some company?"

Sabrina looked at Salem, who stood in the doorway and hung his head contritely. "If you've come up here to beg for your food back, you might as well sit there and do it."

"Okay. I'm begging."

Sabrina pointed the door closed.

"This," Salem called from the other side of the door a moment later, "isn't working out for me at all."

"Welcome to my world."

"You've really had a bad day."

Sabrina flopped back on the bed and stared at the ceiling. "Not really bad. Just confusing."

"Maybe we could talk."

"You just want to talk about you."

"Normally," Salem agreed. "But this afternoon I'll restrain myself."

"Not interested." Sabrina glanced back at the pictures on the bureau. She'd seen her mom a short while ago, when she'd been confused over her feelings toward Harvey and Dashiell, and it had been good to talk to her. But the Career Day assignment just reminded her of how much she missed her mom. *It's just not fair.*

Still, if she had been able to stay with her mom—in some other country, of course—she wouldn't have gotten to know her aunts so well. And then there was that whole bathing out of the canteen thing that sometimes had to be done. *Yuck!*

The Witches' Council had strict guidelines regarding the marriage of witches to mortals. It was frowned upon, and her mom and dad had gone against the rules.

Salem's paw and leg appeared under the door, patting around and scratching haphazardly.

"What are you doing?" Sabrina demanded.

"Cat things," Salem replied. "They're supposed to be cute. Most people cave when they see a cat doing this."

In spite of her mood, Sabrina smiled. "It's better when a kitten does it."

"Pretend I'm young." The paw and leg stayed busy, tapping inquisitively. But the enthusiasm was definitely waning. "Is this working at all? I'm getting tired."

Sabrina pointed the door open.

The cat entered the room and dropped his haunches on the carpet nearby, looking up at the teenage witch. "So maybe you want to tell me what's going on."

"You're feeling like you have to choose between your parents," Salem said when Sabrina finished a few minutes later.

"A little," Sabrina admitted. "Though which parent to choose is a no-brainer under present circumstances."

"You choose your father."

"Right. He's in the book." She pointed to the huge *Discovery of Magic* handbook on its stand at the side of the room. Her father lived in the Witches' Quarter in Paris, France, but she could simply turn to his page to get in contact with him. "I can't have any contact with my mom. It makes me miss her."

"I'm sure she misses you, too," Salem said. "Look on the bright side. The two years is almost up."

"I know. This is just a case of the momentary blues."

"The main thing is to concentrate on what you can do, which is the report." Salem licked his chops. "Too bad about the fashion photographer idea. I found some film and everything."

"Helen would have outclassed it," Sabrina said with a sigh. "You should have seen how big the portfolio she had was."

"I'll bet her photographer wasn't as good as the one you had."

"Well, you're right."

"See, you do have confidence in my abilities. This morning was just a fluke."

"You're right about writing the report," Sabrina amended. "That's what I've got to do." Deciding a course of action made her feel a little better. She got up from the bed and walked over to *The Discovery of Magic* handbook. Opening it, she quickly made her way to her father's page.

Only instead of the smiling picture of Edward Spellman she usually talked to, a yellow banner spread across the space, covering most of her father's face: HI, I'LL BE INCOMMUNICADO FOR A FEW DAYS AND WILL RETURN ON WEDNESDAY. The last line contained an emergency number in Paris.

"He's not there," Sabrina said, closing the book.

"Okay, so you don't have an interview with your dad," Salem said. "It's not the end of the world. Just look up diplomacy in the encyclopedia and wing it from there."

"Not a plan," Sabrina said. "I'm supposed to have quotes about why Dad is doing what he's doing."

"Because the Witches' Council felt he'd be good at it, of course."

Sabrina made a face. "That would look good in the report, wouldn't it?"

"I can see how there'd be a problem." Salem scratched one ear thoughtfully. "You could ask your aunts. After all, they're his sisters. If anyone would know why your dad became a diplomat, they would."

"Maybe you're right." Sabrina pointed up some new clothes, then picked up the cat. "I think they're back."

"Can we make a run by the kitchen?" Salem asked. "I did give you some good advice."

"You did." Sabrina pointed up a treat and fed it to Salem as they walked downstairs.

Chapter 4

"Hey," Sabrina said to Hilda when she stepped into the living room.

"How are you and the great fashion photographer doing?" Hilda asked. She cleared a space on a coffee table and pointed up two soft drinks and a bowl of milk for Salem.

The cat bounded from Sabrina's arms and leaped up onto the table. He lapped the milk noisily then stopped and started gagging. "Fat-free?" *Hack, hack.* "Why would you do something like that?"

"Because I noticed you arrived with Sabrina," Hilda said, "and that tells me you probably talked yourself into a second afternoon snack."

"Actually," Sabrina said, "he didn't. But it wasn't for lack of trying." She sat on the couch.

"What's up?" Hilda asked.

Sabrina sighed. "There's a problem." Sabrina told her aunt about the changes Mrs. Paxton had made in the Career Day assignment. "Since I can't talk to Mom, I thought I'd talk with Dad. Only he's not there."

"I know. Ted had to go away on a business trip for the Witches' Council."

"He told you?" Sabrina asked, feeling puzzled and a little hurt. She and her dad didn't actually talk every day even though they could use magic, but she usually managed to keep up with the things he was doing. "He didn't tell me."

"Actually," Hilda said, "your father didn't tell me. Drell mentioned it when I was talking to him. It's not that big of an assignment, actually, but it's one in a realm where magic communications are kind of spotty."

"Oh." Sabrina felt a little better.

"What did you need to know about your father?" Hilda asked.

"Why did he get involved in the diplomatic corps?"

Hilda smiled proudly. "Ted has always liked to help people out. When we were kids, a lot of times he'd set himself up as mediator when we argued over the rules of a game."

Zelda walked in from the garage holding a cardboard box in her hands. A splotch of grease stained her left cheek. "Ted has always liked to argue," she stated. "Becoming a diplomat for the Witches' Council gave him just the excuse he was looking for."

"That's not it at all," Hilda objected.

"That's exactly it." Zelda put the box on the work booth and pointed up a glass of herbal tea.

"You make it sound like such a—a bad thing."

"No, Ted is actually quite good at arguing," Zelda countered. "Look at the treaty he helped negotiate between the Venusians and the Other Realm a few years back. If he hadn't been willing to argue and stand up for the rights of the witches involved, they would have lost the right to run those concession stands along the seafront."

"But he was looking out for those people," Hilda said.

"True, but that's not why he did it. At least, that's not all of why he did it. The Venusians put up quite an argument. Drell was throwing his hands up at that point."

Sabrina quickly pointed up a legal pad and pen. She wrote furiously. "Wait. Time out. What exactly was the problem between the Other Realm and the Venusians?"

"They were in a dispute over trade agreements, as I recall," Zelda said. "Your dad masterminded the whole thing."

"The Venusians have an agreement with the mortal world," Hilda said, "but I don't know the details of that."

"Sight-seeing tours," Salem piped up, his whiskers drenched in milk. "That's why the alien-abduction craze has gotten so big. The Venusians—and a few other alien planets—offer trips to other galaxies to high-ranking military officials and key government people."

"Salem would know about that," Zelda said.

"There was a rumor that Salem was behind the Roswell incident," Hilda added. "You know, the whole story about the alien bodies discovered in a wrecked spaceship that was later hidden away in Hangar 13 by the American government."

Sabrina nodded, trying to keep up with everything she was being told.

"The rumor was that those bodies and that spaceship were placed out there in the New Mexico desert for the U.S. military to find as an advertising campaign. If the American government had leaked the news to the press, tourism to the other planets would have skyrocketed. No pun intended."

"Those rumors were never confirmed," the cat said.

"Nor were they denied," Hilda said. "The Witches' Council did a partial investigation."

"The problem was," Zelda put in, "that Salem was thought to have been working under the auspices of certain key personnel on the Witches' Council."

"See," the cat said. "Those people aren't without a little shame themselves."

"So you're confirming this?" Sabrina asked.

Salem hesitated. "No. I'm just saying that where there's smoke, there's usually fire."

Both Sabrina's aunts looked at the cat.

"There's been more smoke around me than the

average person," Salem said. "It happens sometimes. I'm just unlucky in love and world domination."

"The Witches' Council diplomatic corps had to step in and chill things out," Hilda said.

"Why?" Sabrina asked.

Zelda shook her head. "Sabrina, the mortal world isn't ready for witches; how can they possibly be ready for meeting alien races?"

"Watching episodes of *Star Trek?*" Sabrina asked.

"Not likely. There are things out there that the Witches' Discovery Corps hasn't encountered yet."

"There's a Witches' Discovery Corps?"

"Yes. They're responsible for mapping out other worlds and other realms. It's a full-time job. You'd be surprised how many there are."

Sabrina tried to focus on her dad and his diplomatic career. She looked at her notes. "Was Dad involved in this Roswell thing?"

"No," Hilda answered. "That was before your father's time."

"The Venusian thing was his, though?"

"Yes. And he was the one who used the loopholes that were generated by the Roswell incident. He also does a lot of campaigning for witches who had one mortal parent, to make sure they get the same help and guidance that witches in the Other Realm get."

"One of the things you'll have to keep in mind, Sabrina," Zelda said gently, "is that you can't get too descriptive about the things your father has done and is doing."

Sabrina looked at her notes, suddenly realizing how much she couldn't tell about her father. "This isn't going to be much of a report, is it?"

Both her aunts frowned sympathetically.

"Yeah," Salem said, "but you could work on mysterious. Everybody loves a mysterious cat. Uh, guy."

"Career Day isn't about mysterious." Sabrina tossed the pad and paper into the air and pointed them away. "It's about informative."

"You could still do a paper about the diplomatic corps," Hilda said.

"Except Dad isn't part of it." Sabrina sighed. "This is driving me crazy. I've got one parent I can't talk to and the other one I can't talk about."

"Willard did say you could pick out someone else who's part of the family," Zelda said.

"Let me guess," Hilda said snidely. "He recommended himself as a subject."

Sabrina nodded.

"I think it's a fine idea," Zelda said. "Unless, of course, you'd prefer to write about something else."

"And there is another positive note," Hilda said with a smile. "You know no one else is going to volunteer to do the Vice Principal Willard Kraft story."

Sabrina glanced at her watch. I've got to get to the library. I'm supposed to meet Harvey there to do some research, then go to the Slicery and compare notes. If that's okay."

"That's fine," Zelda said. "Just make sure you're in by twelve."

Sabrina hugged both her aunts good-bye and left. *Is there any good way to make "I Want to Be a High School Vice Principal Like Mr. Kraft" attractive?* She really didn't think so. Her report was doomed to mediocrity.

☆

Chapter 5

☆

Sabrina looked down one row after another in the Westbridge Municipal Library and felt totally lost. All the stacks were starting to look the same.

She had an armload of books, all of them biographies of famous high school vice principals. Until tonight the teenage witch had thought a famous high school vice principal was an oxymoron.

"Hey, Sab."

Turning around, Sabrina spotted Harvey sitting at one of the nearby tables. "Hi, Harvey. You got here early."

He nodded and grinned. "Yeah, I got excited about my report."

Pest control and crawling through vermin-infested buildings? Sabrina smiled at him. "Maybe you have a fever."

A noise as loud as a leaky radiator hissed from the left. Glancing in that direction, Sabrina spotted Mrs. Acres standing behind a pile of books at the checkout desk. "Shhhhhh," she hissed again. "This is a place of study. No talking out loud." The library crowd was small, although there were a few others from Mrs. Paxton's class cramming the books.

Sabrina nodded, then swung into the seat next to Harvey. "What are you excited about?"

"Pest control," Harvey said. "I was talking to my dad about it tonight. You know, the kinds of training you have to have, the things you have to do. Then he started telling me about the really weird stuff pest-control techs get into."

Sabrina backed away just a moment. "Do I really want to know this?"

Harvey grinned. "Yeah. This is really cool stuff. My dad has this friend who worked as a pest-control tech in New York City." He paused. "I can work it into the paper if it was a friend of my dad's, can't I?"

"I think so," Sabrina answered. "I'm planning on doing that with my paper." *No way can I do a whole report—even a short one—on Mr. Kraft.* That was why she was picking up all the other books she'd found.

"Terrific. I thought so."

"What did your dad tell you about?"

"You're going to absolutely freak when you hear this."

"That's what I'm afraid of. But go ahead." Sabrina felt happy just watching Harvey be happy.

"My dad's friend was working pest control about

42

thirty years ago," Harvey said. "Back then a lot of parents were buying baby alligators for their kids. Lizards and fish are part of the reptile family. They have a tendency not to get any bigger than the containers they live in."

"Biology class," Sabrina said. "I remember."

"Well, these kids kept their pet alligators for a while, but they got bored with them, the way kids will," Harvey continued. "The parents didn't want them and the pet stores wouldn't take them back because the alligator craze had kind of dwindled and everybody had them while nobody wanted them."

"The parents flushed the alligators down the toilet," Sabrina said.

Harvey looked surprised. "You've heard this story?"

"I thought everybody had heard this story. The alligators grew up in the sewers of New York and had to be removed."

"Right." Harvey flipped through the oversize book in front of him.

"I don't think the story about the alligators was true," Sabrina said.

"I know," Harvey said, leafing through the pages. "My dad told me the mayor of New York City wanted everything kept quiet. I was looking through this magazine tonight researching the story. You'd be surprised how much has been kept hidden from the general populace."

Scanning the pages, Sabrina spotted a story about the UFO landing at Roswell, New Mexico. "What are you reading?" she asked.

Harvey closed the book to reveal the cover. "A bound edition of *National Inquisitor.* This is a really cool book, Sab. You wouldn't believe what these guys write."

Most people don't, Sabrina thought, although she didn't say that. "That might not be a good resource."

Shaking his head, Harvey said, "I'm not using it as a resource. What my dad's friend told him is good enough. I just wanted some pictures." He folded the book back and pushed it toward Sabrina.

In the center of the *National Inquisitor* page, a giant alligator scrabbled out of a manhole in the center of a Manhattan street. The huge beast was in the process of overturning a metro bus while army machine gunners fired directly at it. A helicopter hovered overhead.

"Harvey, are you sure you want to use this?" Sabrina asked.

"Sure, Sab." Harvey's eyes twinkled in that way that melted Sabrina's heart. "If I get a color copy of this picture, then add what my dad told me about his friend, I'm going to have one of the coolest Career Day reports." He brandished the picture proudly.

"Except that looks like the army in that picture instead of a pest-control tech."

Harvey waved it away. "They sent the military in by mistake first. Dad's friend told him about that. Then Earl and his team got the call to come take care of business."

"And they took care of business?"

Harvey nodded. "Oh, sure. After all the action they'd seen in Japan with the giant insect invasion there, they handled the alligators in New York like it wasn't anything at all."

"That's good," Sabrina said, giving up. They didn't have much time before the library closed.

"What are you looking for?" Harvey asked. "Maybe I can help."

"A book," Sabrina replied, taking out the piece of paper she'd written the title down on. "I've been stumbling through the library for the last few minutes looking for it. I'm beginning to think the Dewey Decimal System stands for Dewey Find It or Dewey Not?" She sighed.

"What are you doing your report on?"

"Being a high school vice principal."

Harvey grimaced. "Ouch. I can guess who twisted your arm over that one."

"If your guess is Mr. Kraft," Sabrina said, "you win and thanks for playing."

"Hey, can I have that book?"

Sabrina looked up. Olin Ellis, a boy in her class, was standing by her elbow, looking desperate. "Shhh!" the librarian hissed. Olin nodded at the librarian in embarrassment. He reshuffled the tall stack of books she carried and set them on the table by Harvey. They tilted precariously. Only Harvey's quick reflexes kept them from spilling all over the floor.

"Where did you find that book?" Olin asked.

"What book?" Sabrina asked.

Olin touched one of the books in Sabrina's stack. "This one on Hubert Pumperal, the vice principal of

Spartansburg High in Mississippi. I've been looking for it all night."

"You have?" Sabrina asked. "Why?" But a cold feeling of dread was already winding through her stomach because she figured she knew.

"For my report. To get information for my report."

"Who are you doing your report on?" Sabrina asked.

"Mr. Kraft." Olin glanced through the rest of the books in Sabrina's stack. "Oh, I guess you are, too. Maybe we can just share the book."

"I can't believe Olin's doing a report on Mr. Kraft." Sabrina sat at a back table in the Slicery, the pizzeria that was a favorite hangout for Westbridge High students. She stared at Olin. He was ordering pizza.

Crowds gathered around the Foosball tables, leaving little space left over to get through. The noise level from conversations was incredible, blotting out the din of the pinball machines, the jukebox, and the cheering of the Foosball players and onlookers. The sharp tang of pepperoni and hot cheeses filled the air.

"If it's any consolation, when I was talking to him at the library earlier," Harvey said, sitting on a stool beside her, "I don't think Olin could believe it, either."

Sabrina was totally bummed. First, she'd had to view Mr. Kraft as a silver lining, now she was going to have to share him with someone. She couldn't believe she could be so unlucky.

"He did ask him," Harvey said. "Olin didn't go looking for him or anything."

"I know," Sabrina grumped. "But Mr. Kraft is going out with my aunt, not his. His story should be my story."

"You really kind of got into that whole vice principal career thing, didn't you?"

Sabrina sighed. "No, but at least I'd decided on something then." After she'd found out Olin was doing his report on Mr. Kraft, she'd returned her books—except for the one Olin had been looking for.

Olin carried the pizza he'd ordered through the crowd of people, holding it high over his head to keep other people from picking off the meats and veggies. "Okay, things are a little crowded in here even for a Friday night." He laughed nervously. "Um, can I sit here?"

Sabrina nodded, too polite to say no.

Very carefully Olin didn't make eye contact with Sabrina, occupying himself with his pizza wedge.

"I give up," Sabrina said after awhile. "How did Mr. Kraft talk you into it?"

"He didn't talk me into it," Olin replied. "At least, not exactly."

"Fine, give me the inexact story of how it happened." Sabrina felt bad about feeling irritated at her classmate. Olin didn't deserve it, but the teenage witch didn't feel like she deserved all the bad luck she was having.

Olin swallowed a small bite of pizza, almost

choking. "I saw him after school. I guess you were in detention about then."

Terrific, Sabrina thought. *Let's dredge up all the unpleasantness of the day.*

"Mr. Kraft called me over in the hall. He said he thought I looked kind of depressed." Olin nodded. "And he was right, you know. I was feeling bad about having to pick one parent over another for the report. I told him that."

"You could still do a paper on each parent," Sabrina stated.

Olin shook his head. "What if I got a better grade on one of them than the other?"

"Have Mrs. Paxton grade them together." *C'mon! As yucky as it sounds, I've got to have Mr. Kraft as the subject of my report.* Sabrina couldn't believe she felt so desperate.

"I thought about that, but it wouldn't work. I just know I'd do a better job on one of them than the other and they'd know it. Even if they were the same, you know what would happen. One of them would feel like the other one's paper was done better. No, Mr. Kraft is my best hope. He made me realize that today."

How kind and considerate, Sabrina thought. "But I thought this was supposed to be about your parents, at the very least about a family member."

Olin's eyebrows pinched together in suspicion. "Why are you asking about this so much?"

"Because I want to do my report on Mr. Kraft." Sabrina couldn't believe those words had come out of her mouth.

"Oh," said Olin. There was a long pause. "We guess you still can." Olin picked at his pizza, stripping topping and chewing small bites. Sabrina stared, fascinated and repelled. Someone at a nearby Foosball table scored a major goal because the cheering filled the Slicery for a moment. "Then we'd have to see who got to give their report in Mrs. Paxton's class first."

As limited as the subject is, Sabrina realized, *the second person's report will be totally boring.* "I don't think we should both do a report on Mr. Kraft."

"I'm doing my report on Mr. Kraft," Olin stated firmly. He licked pizza sauce off his lip.

"But you can't do that," Sabrina pointed out. "He's not part of your family."

"He's not part of yours, either."

"But he's dating my aunt." All of a sudden, Sabrina felt possessive. *I am really desperate.*

"That just means you'll probably get all the really cool inside stuff." Olin looked sad. "My report won't be able to match yours at all."

Sabrina felt bad, but what else was she going to do? Doing a piece on Swiss clockmakers just didn't sound attractive at all. At least Mr. Kraft had a lot of personal history to work with.

"I've got an idea," Harvey said. "One of you could do Mr. Kraft, the Early Years, and the other could do Mr. Kraft, the Later Years. You know, kind of a two-part paper."

Sabrina and Olin just stared at him.

"You know," Sabrina said, "I'm so desperate, that almost sounds good."

Raising his eyebrows, Harvey smiled and nodded. "See? It's already sounding kind of catchy."

"First dibs on the Later Years," Sabrina said quickly.

Olin looked crestfallen. "Shouldn't we draw numbers or something? I mean, Mr. Kraft's Early Years can't be much to speak of. Did they have cars then?"

"Mr. Kraft? You're fighting over who's going to write a report on Mr. Kraft?"

Recognizing the voice at once, Sabrina felt totally embarrassed. This just was not her day.

☆

Chapter 6

☆

Sabrina glanced over beside the table and saw Helen standing there. "Not exactly," she replied quickly.

"Oh, that's a relief! I couldn't believe you'd stoop to doing a paper about the high school vice principal, Sabrina." Helen giggled.

"Who are you doing your report on, Harvey?" Helen asked.

"My dad. And pest control."

Helen couldn't help grimacing.

"Yeah. It's going to be great." Harvey reached into his pocket and pulled out the color copy he'd made of the *National Inquisitor.* "My dad has a friend who helped get rid of all the alligators in the New York sewers back when that was an epidemic." He pointed to the giant alligator.

Looking at the picture, Helen nodded. "It's kind of tough to beat giant alligators."

Harvey grinned proudly. "That's what I was thinking."

"Well, I've got to be going," Helen said as she walked away.

"That was mortifying," Sabrina said.

"Yeah," Harvey agreed, gazing at the color copy. "She really didn't seem all that impressed by the alligator. And this is one big, ugly alligator. You have to be proud of an alligator like this."

"Do you think Mrs. Paxton will let you do a report on Mr. Kraft?" Sabrina asked Olin.

Olin nodded. "I already asked her. Mr. Kraft told me what to say."

"What did you say?"

"That Mr. Kraft was like a father to me and being a high school vice principal was a job field I'd really be interested in pursuing."

"She bought that?"

Olin nodded. "I think it was because I was desperate. I'm glad you weren't there to hear me." He sighed. "But I really don't want to do my paper on him if you're going to do yours on him. You'll have all the neat stuff he won't tell me."

Neat stuff and Mr. Kraft in the same paper? Sabrina really didn't think so. *I am so pathetic.* She sipped more of her soft drink in misery. "You can do the report on Mr. Kraft."

Olin's face brightened. "Are you sure? I mean, I

know he's more a part of your family than he is of mine."

"I'm positive." Sabrina shrugged and put on a happy face she didn't really feel. "After all, I've got a clock-making career I can write about. What more could you want?" At that point she had to admit that Harvey's alligator was looking pretty good.

"Gosh, thanks, Sabrina!" Olin beamed at her.

Helen was in the center of the Slicery, talking to a growing group of Westbridge students Sabrina recognized from Mrs. Paxton's classes.

"Helen's really getting a lot of attention," Sabrina said.

"It helps if your parent has a really cool job," Harvey said.

Sabrina had to admit she was a little jealous of the attention Helen was getting, even if she was nice. "Yes, it does."

"On Monday Helen's probably going to have all kinds of graphs and reports and visual aids," Harvey said. "And I'm going to have a picture of an alligator."

Sabrina patted him on the arm. "That's one cool alligator, Harvey. Don't feel bad about it."

"You weren't so supportive of it in the library earlier."

"I changed my mind."

"You do that a lot."

"Are you complaining?"

"No. Just noticing."

Sabrina smiled at him, feeling a little better. "I've even got an idea about how to present your alligator. Put it on an overhead viewer sheet and show it on the wall. It'll look huge."

"Yeah, it will. It might even be a little scary."

"Which wouldn't be bad at all." Sabrina laughed. *Monday my report may be pathetic, but hey, tonight I have my friends and a pizza.* She was determined to enjoy herself.

"You know, Sabrina," Harvey said, "you do have a parent with a really cool job."

"My dad's out of town and can't be reached until next Wednesday."

"I'm not talking about your dad." Harvey pulled off a piece of crust. "I'm talking about your mom. She's an archeologist. You know, digging up the past, discovering things no one has seen in thousands or millions of years. Now, that's major cooldom. Not to put your dad's job down, but there are a lot of diplomats in the world, aren't there?"

"Yeah, but my mom—" Sabrina started, then stopped because she couldn't tell them her mom would turn into a ball of wax if she saw her.

"Yeah." Harvey's eyes glittered with excitement. "An archeologist. Kind of like Indiana Jones." He mimed cracking a whip and added sound effects.

"Not like Indiana Jones," Sabrina quickly pointed out. "My mom is, well, she's my mom."

"Has she ever helped discover something really important?" Olin asked.

Sabrina thought back, trying to remember. "I don't know."

"Hasn't she ever talked about her work?"

Guilt filled Sabrina. When she was with her mom, they didn't talk much about her mom's career. "Not much. She only went on a few digs before she and my dad got divorced." *Then a couple years ago, when the possibility that she'd turn into a ball of wax if I saw her came about, she stayed buried in her work. Or, unburying it.*

"Then you don't know if she helped with a major find?" Olin asked.

"No."

"Forget that," Harvey said excitedly. "You ought to find out if she's had to solve any ancient riddles, risk her life climbing perilous cliffs, outwit traps and headhunters, avoid snakes and spiders and—" He paused. "Well, you get the idea."

"Harvey," Sabrina said, "archeological digs are primarily boring and dirty. They're hot and they're cold. There's no television, no friends, and nothing to do except read and dig. That gets old really fast."

"You've been with your mom on digs?" Olin asked.

Sabrina nodded. "When I was little. My dad took me to Mexico to visit with my mom on a dig site near Cancun. I got to visit Tulum, a recovered Mayan city, which was pretty cool. It's built on a cliff thirty-six feet above the ocean. It was absolutely beautiful."

"Have you got any pictures?"

"I think so. You should see the Caribbean Sea. It is *so* blue you just wouldn't believe it."

Olin grimaced. "I wish I had. But see, that's the whole point. A lot of other students probably wish they'd seen places like that. You could write your report and use a lot of pictures that your mom has sent you."

"I don't know if I can find them."

"You know what would be cool?" Harvey asked. "If you found out your mom worked on an archeological dig with an ancient curse, had to slip through torturous traps, and risk their lives to get what they were after. With a couple mysterious deaths thrown in."

Sabrina and Olin looked at him.

Harvey shrugged and returned his attention to the pizza wedge on the small plate in front of him. "I'm just saying that something like that would really get my interest. And it would totally blow Helen's report out of the water."

Images suddenly filled Sabrina's mind. Her mom had sent her a lot of pictures, but she'd only been looking at her mom in them, not at where her mom was or what her mom was doing. *How many people have pictures of their mom digging up dinosaur bones?* She felt reenergized.

As good as Sabrina was feeling, even the prospect of Mr. Kraft picking Zelda up for their weekly date didn't bring her down. "Quotes for my article are going to be a problem. My mom is off in Siberia on a dig, and I can't get in touch with her."

"Oh, yeah," Harvey said. "They uncovered that mammoth in Siberia not too long ago, didn't they? There was a show about it on the Discovery Channel."

Sabrina nodded. "Mom's part of a group that's trying to find a village or something that they think was in the area. But I won't be able to get her to talk to me about her career."

"Under the circumstances," Olin said, "I'll bet Mrs. Paxton won't have a problem with it. After all, your mom probably told you plenty of stuff over the years that you could write down. Archeology isn't like a 'Would you like fries with that?' job. People who do it have a real passion for it."

"You're right." Sabrina felt guilty. Maybe her mom was passionate about archeology, but she'd never really listened for that in her mom's voice. Her mom, for the most part, had just been her mom. "Thanks, Olin," she said.

It wasn't until Sabrina had had to make the decision between Dashiell and Harvey and had gotten the chance to talk to her mom that she started realizing how real her mom was. The prospect of digging into her mom's career was suddenly really appealing.

"What are you looking for?"

Sabrina glanced at her aunts. They stood in the doorway to her bedroom wearing shocked expressions. The teenage witch couldn't blame them. Photo albums, pictures, and boxes of souvenirs and keepsakes lay strewn across her bedroom.

"I figured out who I'm doing my Career Day report on." Sabrina took a dusty box from the top of her bedroom closet. A cloud of dust swirled around her and made her sneeze. "Wow, I've got to get up there more often and do some cleaning." She placed the box on the littered bed and started searching.

"Who?" Zelda asked.

"My guess is the sanitation department," Salem commented. The cat sat on the floor between the aunts with his tail wrapped around himself. "The guys who do the emergency rescue salvage jobs. Or maybe FEMA, the Federal Emergency Management Agency, because this room could be declared a disaster area."

Salem was right, Sabrina had to admit. Boxes sat on every available surface in the room, as well as the floor. Pictures stood in stacks of yeses, noes, and maybes. She'd even tried to group them according to country going by the notations her mother had made on their backs.

"It's not as bad as it looks." Sabrina found another packet of pictures. She rifled through them, thinking maybe they were from someplace in Europe. *Wow, Mom really gets around.* For a moment, she considered what life might have been like if she'd gotten to live with her mom instead of going to live with her aunts. She could have seen so many places, met so many people.

But then, there was that whole bathing out of a canteen thing to think of.

"This room is every bit as bad as it looks," Hilda said. "This is grounds for, well, grounding."

"It's for school," Sabrina said. "Consider it an excavation. I've decided to do my report on my mom and being an archeologist."

"Why, Sabrina, what a great idea," Zelda enthused. She crossed the room, cleared a spot on the bed, and started going through the pictures, journals, and letters as well. "I'm glad you hung on to all the things your mother has sent you over the years."

"Me, too. It's going to make writing this report easy. Except for the interviewing part."

"I think you can figure out enough to write about your mom from all this." Zelda flipped through the pictures. "I've always thought your mother's career was fascinating."

"You did?" Sabrina was surprised. She'd never heard either of her aunts speak of her mother with anything other than high regard even after the divorce, but she hadn't known Zelda had possessed an interest in her mom's career.

"Yes, and so did your father."

"Ted met your mom on a dig in Egypt," Hilda added, looking at her sister. "There was some kind of mummy or ancient curse involved in that site, wasn't there?"

"A mummy?" Sabrina's interest pricked up immediately. This was getting better all the time. "An ancient curse?"

Chapter 7

☆

"Curses, schmurses, this was in Egypt." Salem padded across the room and stretched up to reach the bed. He pulled himself up onto the bed gently and sprawled across a half-dozen journals. "How could you go to that country and not hear about ancient curses and mummies? Egypt positively reeks of them. Why, I remember one time—"

"Quiet, Salem," Zelda said. "Sabrina wants to talk about her mom."

"Well, it was an interesting story," Salem groused.

"Tell me about the curse and the mummy," Sabrina said.

"I don't know that there was a whole lot to tell," Zelda said. "I remember your mother writing to me about it, but she was confused a little herself. The archeological expedition she was on had gotten permission from the Egyptian government to excavate a tomb in the Valley of the Kings."

"Your dad was there as a liaison for the American ambassador to Egypt," Hilda said. "I remember talking to him the day he met your mom."

"What was Dad doing on the dig site?" Sabrina couldn't imagine her elegantly clad father traipsing around sand dunes with any kind of eagerness.

"A young assistant at the dig discovered Menkhotep's lost tomb," Zelda replied.

Sabrina felt puzzled. "Aren't they all lost? Isn't that the reason for going and looking for them?"

"There are records, of course," Zelda said. "The archeological expeditions use them to make educated guesses about where the tombs might be. But the cost of the excavations is extremely expensive."

"The Egyptian government doesn't allow anyone to take artifacts out of the country," Salem said. "They're very testy about that. And that brings me to another tale."

"We'll leave that one for later as well," Hilda said.

The cat pouted.

"Menkhotep was a lesser-known figure in Egyptian royalty," Zelda went on. "Your mother did a couple of monographs on Menkhotep later, but the find wasn't of major importance as far as the rest of Egyptology was concerned."

"It wasn't?"

"Menkhotep was very secretive. There are people

in Egypt today who keep the records your mother and Dr. Mellon's expedition discovered."

"Why?"

Zelda shrugged. "Your mother never found out, but she assumed it was because of the mummy's curse."

"The mummy's curse." Sabrina savored the sound of that. Her excitement grew. "So why was Dad there?"

"A powerful lobbying group in Egypt wanted to cancel the dig," Zelda said. "Your father was asked to intervene in the matter and did so successfully."

"Can you tell me anything else?"

"As I recall, there were tomb raiders involved."

Oh, man, this story just keeps getting better. "Tell me about the tomb raiders."

"They were after Menkhotep's treasure," Zelda said. "There was a rumor Menkhotep had discovered the secret of eternal youth."

"Now, there's a big seller," Salem commented. "You'd be surprised how many times you can sell the same old tired map to people looking for the secret of eternal youth." He blinked owlishly when he found himself the center of the attention of all three witches. "Not that I'd know from personal experience. I've just heard stories."

"What happened with the tomb raiders?" Sabrina asked.

"It's been a long time," Zelda said. "Before you were born even. What I can do is give you the scrapbook I made out of the letters and pictures your mother sent me." She pointed. Immediately a large leather-bound book appeared in her hands. "Here it is."

"Personally," Hilda commented, pointing up a cup of hot cocoa that she handed to Sabrina, "I've always found your mother's job to be somewhat gruesome."

"I thought you liked scary things," Sabrina said.

Hilda shook her head and pointed up a cup of hot cocoa for herself. "There's scary and there's gruesome. Now, a zombie, that's scary. Going into a tomb with a magnifying glass, that's gruesome." She shuddered. "Hanging out at the cemetery to see who pops up is fun, but not if you have to go dig them up yourself."

"I'm sure there's a difference, but right now I really don't want to know," Sabrina said.

"Your mother has had an interesting career," Zelda commented. She opened the scrapbook to reveal a dozen photographs taped onto the page.

Sabrina scanned the pictures, seeing her mom in jodhpurs and tall boots in the African veldt, canoeing in underground rivers lighted only by flashlights, hiding up in a tree while menaced by bears below, and standing in an open tomb with an unopened sarcophagus. There was so much to see that she couldn't believe she hadn't seen it before.

"Mom really did all of this?" She turned the pages, flipping through the images.

"Every bit of it," Zelda said. "Your mother has led a very adventurous life. That's one of the things that attracted your father to her."

"They met in Egypt while she was looking for this Menkhotep's tomb?" Sabrina kept turning pages.

"Yes. Of course, I didn't get the pictures till after she and Ted were married, but I remember Ted talking about her. She made quite an impression on him." Zelda flipped to another section of the scrapbook.

Pictures of Sabrina's mom kneeling in the middle of a desert with a trenching tool, in low, winding tunnels walled up by rocks, and standing with her flashlight pointing down at an ornate sarcophagus covered the pages. Newspaper articles in English and at least three other languages showed grainy pictures in black and white. Some of the photographs of her mom were in black and white, but Sabrina knew that was because black-and-white film often picked up greater detail than color film.

Sabrina paused at one of the pictures on the next page. It showed her mom and dad standing together in front of a pitched tent with a sun flap over them. Her dad wore an immaculate white suit while her mom was dressed in khaki shorts and shirt. She held a pith helmet in one hand, and a red bandanna tied around her head kept the hair from her eyes.

"They look like they were really in love," Sabrina said.

"They were," Hilda said. "After that meeting, your dad didn't stop talking about your mom. They stayed in touch, and your dad arranged it so he could go visit her on a couple other digs. It was no surprise when they got married a few months later."

Sabrina looked at the young couple. It wasn't hard to imagine her and Harvey looking like that, with goofy grins on their faces. "Why did Mom get so interested in archeology?"

"She never said," Zelda replied.

"Never?" Sabrina frowned. *Now, there's an obvious hole in my Career Day report. No, that's not a hole, that's a crater.*

"I think it was just something she fell in love with," Zelda answered. "Like your dad."

"Wait!" Sabrina cried. "That can't be the answer. That's not going to look good in Mrs. Paxton's report. *Because* isn't an answer that's supposed to work in the adult world."

"I'm sorry, dear, that's the only answer I have. We never talked about why she did what she did, only about what. Your mom is a very interesting person." Zelda handed Sabrina the scrapbook. "It might be better if you looked through your mother's things and came up with your own conclusion."

Sabrina looked at all the pictures and journals covering her bed. She wanted to groan. The task ahead looked enormous.

Zelda stood and surveyed the bed herself. "It does appear somewhat daunting, doesn't it?"

"Yes."

"Just bear in mind that what you're looking for isn't one specific thing, Sabrina," Zelda advised. "You're just looking for your mother's motivation to do the work she does. If you look with that in mind, you're going to find that it's in everything she does."

"I hope so."

"You could wait until tomorrow and start on it fresh," Hilda said. "Cable is running the *Ghouls' Night Out* special tonight. I've got some munchies in the fridge."

Salem gathered himself and erupted from the bed, leaping to the floor. "I'm there."

"I think I'm going to pass," Sabrina said. "This job looks bigger than I thought it would be. If I get lucky, I can at least get things organized."

Salem chuckled maniacally. "More for me! Bwaaa-haaa-haaaa!"

Sabrina thanked her aunts for their time and the offer, and turned her attention back to the debris strewn across her bed.

Lying back on the bed with a reading lamp glowing over her shoulder, Sabrina read through her mother's journals. She was searching for the Egyptian mummy mystery, but she kept getting sidetracked with the different stories her mother had written in her journals about other archeological digs. One of the things the teenage witch had discovered about her mother was that she really knew how to tell stories. She'd gotten started on several entries and hadn't been able to put them aside until she finished reading those sections.

Downstairs, she heard the roar of a ghoul in full

attack mode and terrified screams, followed almost immediately by Hilda's and Salem's laughter.

At the moment, however, Sabrina was deep in the Amazonian rain forest hunting for the ruins of a lost Inca city.

Looking out over the crushing weight of the trees and underbrush of the mountainous foothills we had to cross, Dr. Gordon decided that our only option was the aerial travel Hector Royo, our guide, advised.

Royo guided us to a tall conifer that towered at least a hundred and fifty feet from the ground. He quickly scaled up the rope ladders attached to the tree, stopping to mend the ones that were broken or rotted through.

During the course of our journey overland on the forest floor so far, Royo had taught me some of the more common knots his people used. I had no problem climbing up and helping him mend them.

"My mom?" Sabrina mused to herself. "A hundred and fifty feet off the ground in a tree, hanging from rotting and broken rope ladders? No way." She couldn't help reading even though it wasn't the story she was looking for.

Once we had the ladders repaired, we had a pretty easy time of it—except for Dr. Browne, who wasn't quite in shape to be playing monkey in the treetops.

Standing at the top of the conifer, I gazed down at the Amazonian rain forest spread out below me. Although I'd been around the rain forest a few times before, I'd never been in a section this old and this tall. It was breathtaking.

We were in the emergent layer of the rain forest now. This was the part where primarily butterflies and eagles lived. To get from place to place in the emergent layer, creatures that lived there needed to be able to fly. We couldn't fly, but we did have the zip lines Royo led us to.

The zip lines were cables outfitted with wheeled seats that carried us over areas we'd have had to cut our way through with machetes. Royo assured us the wheeled seats were safe and well taken care of, but it was somewhat unsettling—to say the least!—to go whizzing across spaces well over a hundred feet high.

[Note to self: Be prepared to discuss the three other parts of the rain forest, including the canopy layer, the understory, and the forest floor itself. I think these would be good research areas for budding botanists looking for class projects. Ha-ha!]

We made the trek that afternoon without trouble, trusting Royo to pick out the lines we traveled along and repair any that needed attention. Only a few hours later, very worn out and very much in need of baths, we arrived at the ruins.

Reluctantly Sabrina stuck another bookmark in the journal and turned more pages. The familiar thumping weight on the foot of her bed drew her attention.

Salem kneaded the comforter, making a soft spot. He curled his tail around himself and lay down. "Well, you missed a great *Ghouls' Night Out.*"

"So I heard."

"Oh, were we disturbing you?"

"Not really. I was pretty much lost in Mom's journals."

"Making any progress?" Salem yawned, his pink tongue lolling out for a long moment.

"There is so much I didn't know about my mom. Did you know she was once trapped in a pit filled with tarantulas?"

Salem shivered. "No, and I really don't want any more horrible images like that before I go to sleep."

"She stayed in that pit for three hours before the other archeologists could organize a rescue team. She's amazing."

Salem rolled on the bed and stretched. "It's good that you're getting to see this side of your mom."

"I know. I just wish I could see more of it." Sabrina picked up another journal. Each of them was numbered, but she hadn't quite figured out what the coding on the spine meant. She was certain it had to do with the time and place her mother had been. Her mom was just too organized not to keep files in an orderly fashion. "It's also frustrating because I'm reading all these entries but she never just comes out and says what made her want to be an archeologist."

"Maybe she couldn't think of anything else she'd rather be," Salem volunteered. "It was kind of like that with me and world domination. I mean, I got to looking around, thinking how easy it would be since television had come so far in such a short time, and I——"

"Here it is!" Sabrina held the small, scuffed gray notebook in her hands, flipping through the pages excitedly. Her mother's neat script filled the unlined pages with times, dates, and places. Diagrams and drawings broke up the text, showing objects, pyramids, and tunnels.

There were also some caricatures of Dr. Edmund Dodge, the dig's leader, and others her mom had gotten to know. The small, artistic drawings were one of the first things Sabrina had appreciated about her mother's notebooks. She'd had a vague recollection of the pictures her mom used to draw, mainly cartoon figures Sabrina had liked as a child, but she'd never wondered how her mom came to develop the skill.

Other pages held drawings of the finds they'd made. Hieroglyphics, some of them with translations on facing pages, occupied other pages. There were even maps of the areas the dig party had been in.

The journal began with the archeological party's landing in Cairo at the international airport. Sabrina read the journal avidly, enjoying her mom's attention to detail.

Her mom and the dig team had stayed in one of the city's smaller hotels for the night, enjoying a final restaurant meal before taking the nearly five-hundred-mile train trip to Luxor the next morning. Her mom had even listed what she'd had for dinner.

So much detail, Mom, Sabrina thought, *but why didn't you ever write about why you went?* She kept reading.

Dr. Edmund Dodge was a little different from what I was expecting. I'd known about his education in Oxford, and of his excavations of the Iron Age and Roman sites in England, so I guess I'd prepared myself for a no-nonsense kind of taskmaster.

When he greeted us at the train station in Luxor, he was full of good humor and even had a picnic lunch on hand for us. After getting all our personal things loaded onto the jeeps and trucks he'd commandeered for our trip to the West Bank, we were off.

Excitement filled me. Egyptology had been of interest all my life. When I was a little girl back home, I used to round up friends in the neighborhood to go on archeological digs. We traipsed along spring streams looking for pirates' treasure. And we dug in local development areas going from maps I'd draw trying to find a mummy's tomb.

This whole expedition to find Menkhotep's lost tomb was something I'd dreamed of all my life. I couldn't wait. My sandwich got stale as I stared out the window and listened to Dr. Dodge speak about the history of the Valley of the Kings. I felt like I was on the greatest adventure of my life!

If things worked out and our information was correct, we'd soon be able to claim the mummy of Menkhotep despite the curse that was supposed to be laid over the tomb!

Chapter 8

"**N**o!" Sabrina wailed.

At the foot of the bed, Salem woke with a start, pawing the air in fear. "What, what? No, I swear I'll put it back! I was only looking at it! I would never—" The cat caught himself and stopped suddenly. He glanced at Sabrina. "Nightmare. I would never actually—never mind."

Sabrina closed the scuffed gray journal and put it across her knees.

"I'm going to take a guess here," the cat said, "and bet there was a reason why you woke me."

"Sorry," Sabrina apologized, "but this is so not cool."

Salem rolled over onto his stomach. "I understand. Can it keep till morning? We're in the early A.M. here."

"This is just horrible."

73

Blinking at the journal Sabrina held, Salem said, "Before I went to sleep, you were happy."

"Now I'm not."

"I got that part. I think what I'm missing is why."

"I don't want to talk about it."

Salem stretched. "Good. I mean, turn out the light and we can talk about it in the morning."

"I can't just not talk about it," Sabrina said. "I'm upset."

"I'm confused."

"Me, too."

"Maybe this is something you should talk about with your aunts," Salem suggested.

"I don't want to wake them."

"But you can wake the cat?"

"You're in here," Sabrina said, "and you nap all the time."

"I'm not napping now."

"It's this journal," Sabrina said.

"The one about the mummy?"

Sabrina nodded. "There's so much buildup about the whole Menkhotep thing, then nothing."

"Nothing?"

"Mom and the dig party found the mummy," Sabrina said. "But there's a lot of the story missing. She ends up talking about Dad a lot, which is kind of creepy reading how your mom felt about your dad, but she leaves out a lot about Menkhotep."

She'd felt a little uncomfortable reading some of the passages because it was a little like spying on her parents. But after a while she realized that her mom's feelings for her dad were a lot like the ones she had for Harvey. It was kind of nice and reassuring after a while.

"So you've got daddy but no mummy," Salem said.

"Not much mummy," Sabrina agreed. "Not nearly enough mummy for the kind of paper I want to present to Mrs. Paxton's class."

"If they found the mummy," Salem asked, "isn't that kind of the end of the story?"

"It's the end, but there's a lot of the middle left out. You can tell from the way Mom was writing. The later entries, except for most of the ones about Dad and how he helped the dig party out with the Egyptian government, are kind of brief."

"Maybe your mom was tired."

"No. I've been reading her journals, Salem. Mom has always been very detailed and painstaking."

"So what do you think happened?"

"I'm wondering if someone made her be quiet about some things."

"Like what?"

"I have no idea."

Salem stretched again, rippling his back. "I think maybe you've been watching *Conspiracies Today* a little too much."

"You watch that show, not me."

The cat blinked. "Oh, yeah."

Sabrina got up from the bed. "Come on."

"Come on?" The cat remained on the bed.

"I want to talk about this."

Salem shook his head. "No way. I'm tired. Talking about mummies in the mortal world is boring for the most part, and any discussion of how they were prepared is totally nauseating. Just thinking about those little pliers and tools, and the jars with—" He stopped and shivered. "Bleah!"

"I'll bet some of Hilda's treats are still in the fridge," Sabrina coaxed.

"Hold up," Salem called.

Downstairs in the kitchen Sabrina served the left-over Coconut Zombie Fingers cookie bars Hilda had prepared for the movie earlier. Her aunt had even taken the time to paint grimy fingernails on in purple and black icing.

The teenage witch pointed up a cup of hot cocoa for herself and a saucer of milk for the cat. Then she filled Salem in on what she'd been reading.

The notebook passages had continued on after the arrival in Luxor, detailing the caravan trip and the other people Sabrina's mom had met. At first, there'd been only two or three passages written a day. Then, as the dig progressed and the tomb was actually found by a young student by accident, the passages increased to ten or twelve a day, some of them devoted solely to one or two items they'd found.

"There wasn't much detail about the mummy, huh?" Salem nibbled on a corner of a Coconut Zombie Finger. Sabrina had sprinkled shredded bacon on his.

Opening the journal, Sabrina fanned through the pages at the back of the book. She found a drawing of Menkhotep's sarcophagus. The detail, as usual in her mom's drawings, was very complete.

"There's a lot of detail about the find," Sabrina said. "But not much mention of the curse."

"Maybe the curse was a myth."

Sabrina sipped her hot cocoa. She felt really tired, but she knew she couldn't sleep. Her excitement and curiosity over the dig wouldn't let her rest. "I need to know."

"For the Career Day paper?" Salem shook his head. "You've probably got everything you need to know for that."

"I want the mummy." Sabrina thought about the presentation. "And I want to be first to give my paper to the class. I want Helen squirming in her chair, knowing she has to follow me."

"Are there any other journals about the mummy?"

"None that I've found so far, and most of the journals I haven't gone through in detail are from later times. It wasn't unusual for Mom to make notes even years later if some bit of research led her to new conclusions about something she'd found or seen earlier. But I haven't seen anything further about the mummy."

"That could be because there was nothing further."

"I think there was. My intuition—"

"May just be wishful thinking."

Sabrina paused. "There's one way to find out."

"Ask your Mom?"

"I can't do that. Communication between us is forbidden, remember?"

"You could wait till the two years are up," Salem suggested.

"The Career Day paper is due before then." Sabrina paused. "The only way to know for sure what happened is to go back there and find out."

"You mean back *then*."

Sabrina shrugged. "There, then. Whatever."

"I don't know, Sabrina. Time travel is a tricky thing."

"It's not like it's my first time to time travel."

"No, but now you're messing around with your own personal history. Suppose you say or do something that affects how your mom acts?"

"That's not going to happen."

"Sure, and that's what everybody says. Time travel is a lot of fun till you go and get yourself unborn."

"I've got to go do this." Sabrina cleared the dishes from the table with a point.

"Your aunts will ground you if you're caught."

"I won't get caught."

Salem blinked at her. "You're telling me. Usually when people tell me secrets, their next move is to throw themselves on the mercy of the court."

"I need you here," Sabrina said. "In case something goes wrong."

"If something goes wrong," the cat told her, "I won't even remember who you are. There's no reset button on a time-travel spell."

"I'll leave a note."

"You can't leave a note if you're unborn. You were never here to do it."

Sabrina thought furiously, trying to remember all the time-travel movies she'd watched with Harvey. "I'll leave a message in a bottle where Hilda and Zelda can find it."

"Oh, that works fine if you get stuck back in time," Salem said, "but getting unborn is a whole new kettle of fish." He licked his chops. "Which isn't an entirely bad thought. I really need to work on unattractive metaphors."

"I'm going." Sabrina's mind was made up. She had to know the whole story of the mummy.

"Then there's that whole Mom-turning-into-a-ball-of-wax thing to worry about."

"I thought about that." Sabrina started up the stairs to her room. "But since I'm traveling back in time, I won't be seeing her during the two-year period. I won't even be seeing her while I'm alive. Technically."

"And you're sure this is going to work?" Salem climbed the stairs beside her.

"Of course I'm sure." Sabrina smiled at the cat, feeling extremely confident. "If this wasn't going to work, a future me would have popped into now and told me not to go, right?"

"You know," Salem said, "that's scary. It makes a lot of sense in a twisted sort of way that I find very reassuring."

"Thank you."

"Unless you got yourself unborn. In which case, you wouldn't be around to come back and tell your past self—you—not to go."

"But if I accidentally got myself unborn, I

wouldn't be here now, would I? Unless you want to factor in the whole can of worms about the possibility of alternate time-lines."

"Stop! You're making my head hurt! I hate this stuff!"

Sabrina stood in front of her mirror, holding up one of the pictures of her mom. She pointed up a new outfit that looked a lot like her mom's. The khaki shorts and shirt felt a little rough, but they looked good. She took a moment and pointed up a pack as well, basing it on the description of contents that had been in the journals.

Returning to the bed, she picked up her mom's journal regarding the Menkhotep dig and stuck it into her pack.

"Sabrina," Salem said, lying on the bed, "I can't let you go alone."

Suddenly feeling as if someone had poured ice water in her veins, Sabrina said, "You're not going." When it came to travel, trouble seemed to follow her cat everywhere.

"You don't have a choice," Salem told her. "A couple of yowls from me and your aunts will come running."

"I could gag you," Sabrina warned.

"I still know Morse code, and so does Zelda. Nope, you have no option but to let me go, too."

Sabrina considered the situation, trying to find some way out of it. She'd had to tell Salem for just the reason she'd given him: in case she got into trouble, she needed her aunts to know.

"You're going to let me go," Salem reasoned, "because your future self isn't here telling you that it's a mistake to let me go."

"That's because the present me already knows it's a mistake. No news flash there."

"So," the cat said, "are we going or not?"

"Going," Sabrina said. And to tell the truth, she was glad Salem insisted on going. As she'd gotten ready, she realized how much she didn't want to go alone. She was going to be in a strange country with people she didn't know and potential danger. *Even more danger than just the possibility of getting unborn. Although, that's a pretty big worry!*

She pointed at the cat, dressing him in a small khaki shirt and a tiny pith helmet that would have served as a drink coaster. Then she gathered him up in her arms.

"You gotta love Egypt," Salem commented. "The people there really know how to treat a cat."

Pointing at the mirror, Sabrina recited the spell she'd looked up in her *Discovery of Magic* handbook.

Mirror, mirror, on the wall,
Time is like a big beach ball.
The future curves into the past,
So take us there and make it fast.

When she finished the spell, sparkles sprayed from her finger and splashed over the mirror's surface. The mirror image wavered like a memory sequence on a sit-com, then came into focus again.

The image showed a stretch of desert sand fronting a train station. Magical blue script appeared in the middle of the mirror, reading LUXOR, EGYPT. The time was the day before Menkhotep's tomb had been found.

Sabrina took a deep breath, then she stepped through the mirror into the past.

Chapter 9

Sabrina trudged across the desert sand, feeling her boots slip and slide as the uncertain footing shifted again and again. The sun was in the east, so she knew it was still morning, but the temperature was already well over a hundred degrees.

Although she'd only been walking a few minutes, she felt bone-tired. The backpack felt impossibly heavy and it didn't help that she had to carry Salem because the sand burned the cat's paws.

She peered across the remaining distance to the train tracks entering Luxor from Cairo to the north. Rising heat waves distorted her view to the point that she didn't know how much farther it was to the warehouse the archeological crews were using to ship and receive goods.

"I'm hot," Salem growled.

"So am I," Sabrina said. "And I'm all sweaty and icky." She wished she'd been able to sleep, maybe even start out in the morning. But that hadn't really been an option because her aunts would have been around.

"You want to tell me why we're going to this warehouse when you could have just zapped us to the dig site?"

"I'd rather save my breath. I'm walking for two, you know."

"It's just that it sounds kind of stupid to walk all this way." Salem moved in Sabrina's arms, trying to find a more comfortable position.

"Stop squirming. You're making it even harder to carry you."

"Whatever happened to 'He's not heavy, he's my cat?' "

"I lost the mood a mile or so back." Sabrina took a deep breath of the overheated air and felt momentarily light-headed.

"Uh-oh. Lunch on the wing." Salem looked up.

Shielding her eyes from the sun even though she had sunglasses on, Sabrina glanced up to see a trio of circling buzzards. "Maybe they're thinking lunch on the hoof."

"Lie down and play dead," Salem suggested. "I can take them. We can cover them in aluminum foil, bury them in the sand for an hour or so, and have baked bird just falling off the bone."

"If I lie down, I don't think I'm getting up again."

Salem glanced at her. "You don't look so good. Maybe you need a drink."

"A drink, a bath, a hotel with room service." Sabrina stopped for a moment, feeling her legs tremble from all the walking. *I should have gotten closer to the warehouse.*

She took the canteen from her hip and unscrewed the cap. It was a good thing the canteen was covered in fabric because she thought it would have burned her fingers otherwise. When she poured water into her cupped palm, Salem lapped it up. The water was hot and tepid.

"At least it was wet," Sabrina said when she put the canteen back on her hip and started walking again.

"Maybe a cactus would be cooler," the cat said.

"I haven't seen a cactus." Sabrina glanced up and spotted the circling vultures again. They were definitely staying with them.

"Are you sure we're going the right way?"

Sabrina checked the compass on her wrist. "Yes. Besides that we're following the train tracks." She walked up a rise she hadn't even noticed because the sand was deceiving, leaning into the incline. She almost fell twice, and started thinking maybe she could finish her paper without the information on the mummy and the curse. But if there was a chance to see her mom, she really wanted to do that, too.

At the top of the rise, the distortion by the heat waves went away. Hossam's Surplus stood less than a hundred yards away on the same side of the tracks Sabrina approached from.

The building appeared ramshackle, made of sun-faded and warped wood that had turned a nasty shade of gray over the years. Nearly a dozen jeeps and cargo trucks were parked haphazardly out front. A single boom arm off-loaded cargo from a huge truck with tires that looked as tall as Sabrina.

"Civilization," Salem gasped.

"Shade," Sabrina croaked. Even though she'd sipped the water, her mouth tasted like sand and felt completely dry. *Why would anyone come here if they didn't have to?* She barely made it the rest of the distance to the warehouse. She leaned against the wall, trying to breathe the thin air.

"Something Orabi can do for you, missy?"

Sabrina hadn't realized she'd closed her eyes until she was spoken to. She turned and glanced at the young man peering at her with concern. He was short and thin, with two gold teeth in front, dressed in a white shirt and pants. "I'm looking for Dr. Edmund Dodge," she said.

Orabi nodded and smiled more broadly. "Ah, yes. Dr. Dodge here. Getting new generator he waiting for. You come, yes?"

"Yes." Sabrina shoved herself forward.

"He expecting you?" Orabi started out taking long strides, then slowed down when he saw that she wasn't keeping up.

"It's a surprise." According to her mother's journal, Dr. Dodge had traveled back to Luxor to pick up a replacement generator for one the dig site had lost three weeks before. Her mom and the others had already been working the excavation for nearly two months.

"Surprises nice, yes?" Orabi grinned again.

Sabrina followed the young man past trucks and jeeps being manually loaded by warehouse workers. Most of them from construction companies. At the front of the warehouse she had her first look at the slow-moving brown water of the Nile River.

Caught up in the moment, amazed by the small size of the river that had nurtured cities for thousands of years, Sabrina just stared.

"First time see Nile River, yes?" Orabi asked.

"First time," Sabrina agreed. "I just didn't expect it to be so small."

"You come dry season," Orabi told her. "In rainy season, river much big. One time I see it flood into warehouse. Old Hossam own warehouse. He experience much unhappiness then. Many, many things get wet. Rice swell up very big." He spread his hands as far apart as he could to show how big.

"I'm sure." Sabrina had a hard time imagining that. She followed the line of the river with her gaze, tracking it on into Luxor. She could just make out the waterfront in the distance.

"Hey," Salem said, "those are cruise ships."

Orabi turned around. "You say something, missy?"

Sabrina waved a hand at the people around her. "Not me. It must have been someone else."

The young man appeared uncertain for a moment. "Okay." He headed on into the warehouse.

Sabrina kept Orabi in sight but lagged far enough

behind to whisper to Salem without being over-heard. "No talking."

"You could have zapped us to a cruise ship," the cat sobbed. "Banquets. Entertainment. You could have called Dr. Dodge from one of them."

"Quiet. I'll bet there are a lot of people around here who'd love to have a talking cat." It felt immediately cooler inside the dark warehouse, but it still wasn't the cool of Westbridge Sabrina was used to. The dimness caused her to take her sunglasses off, and even then the big warehouse was almost too dark to see well. Electric lights hung from the ceiling, bright enough to let people know they were there.

She followed Orabi around stacks of crates and boxes to a small office in the back where two men were seated on opposite sides of a small scarred desk. She recognized Dr. Dodge at once from the caricature in her mother's journal.

The man was probably in his forties, tall and lean, smooth-shaven with his long brown hair pulled back in a ponytail. Despite his deep tan, there was a flush of sunburn under his skin. He wore khaki shorts and a white shirt.

Orabi knocked politely on the door. Both men inside looked up. "Someone here to meet Dr. Dodge, yes," Orabi announced.

Dr. Dodge glanced up. "Do I know you?"

"Not yet," Sabrina said, stepping into the room. "My name is—" She hesitated. *I can't give him my real name.* "—is Bri. Bri Kinkle." That won't be too hard to remember. She offered her hand.

Taking her hand, Dr. Dodge stood and smiled at her. "It's a pleasure to meet you, Miss Kinkle, but I must profess some curiosity as to why you were looking for me."

"Of course you have to profess," Sabrina said. "You're a professor, right?"

"That I am."

Dr. Dodge's smile wasn't as big as Sabrina had hoped for. Back home, before she'd stepped through the mirror, she'd thought briefly of how she was going to introduce herself. "I came out here to be with you on the Menkhotep dig."

"I must say I'm surprised. There are no few fellow academians who believe I'm on something of a snipe hunt following that little piece of legend."

"They're wrong," Sabrina said.

Dr. Dodge laughed. "It's good to hear a show of faith."

"It's just that I believe in your work. That's why, when I talked to one of your students at the university, I wanted to come."

"You're an archeology student? I find it odd that I don't remember you."

"I'm new," Sabrina said. "I haven't taken any of your classes yet."

"Ah, an undergraduate."

"Yes, sir."

"Might I ask how you got out here?"

"I flew into Cairo and took a train to Luxor."

"She walk to warehouse from desert," Orabi said. Sabrina wished the young man would mind his own business. Still, she smiled and said, "I guess I should say I was on the train for a while. I went outside this morning to get a breath of fresh air and fell off the train."

"Good gosh!" the professor exploded, suddenly looking at her more closely. "Were you injured?"

"No," Sabrina answered. "I fell in the sand. There's a lot of it out there."

"Yes, there is. You've been very lucky so far, young lady. Who sent you here?"

"No one. I came because I wanted to."

"You paid for the trip yourself?"

"I really wanted to come," Sabrina said.

Dr. Dodge flicked his gaze down at Salem. "And you brought your cat?"

"Actually, this is a stray I found this morning." Salem flicked his claws out just enough to sting.

"In the desert?"

Sabrina nodded. "He kind of got attached to me. Won't leave me."

"Probably because you fed him, missy," the man on the other side of the desk said. He opened his desk and took out a box of kitty treats. He held one between his fingers.

Before Sabrina could stop him, Salem was out of her arms and onto the desktop. He gratefully accepted the kitty treat and purred loudly.

The man behind the desk laughed. "This one doesn't appear skinny enough to be a true stray. Perhaps he belongs to someone."

"I'm sorry, Bri. This is Hossam. He owns this

place, and you won't meet a kinder, more gentle thieving rascal in all your life."

Hossam stood and bowed. "A pleasure, missy. Orabi, get back to work."

The young man tossed a quick salute and disappeared back into the warehouse.

"Maybe I should keep your new friend here and try to find his owner," Hossam offered.

Salem's eyes rounded. He glanced a final time at the box of kitty treats the warehouse owner still had, then rapidly trotted across the desk and leaped into Sabrina's arms.

"I guess maybe he wants to stick with me for a while," Sabrina said. Salem purred dramatically.

"As you wish." Hossam resumed his seat.

"So how about it?" Sabrina asked Dr. Dodge. "Can you use another pair of hands on the dig?"

"Young lady, I'd hate to think you parted with all that money and time only for me to send you packing," Dr. Dodge said. "Also, an archeological dig is always lacking in a few areas, manpower often being one of them. How much experience do you have?"

"Well, I've dug up a few flower beds."

The professor laughed. "Seriously now."

Sabrina thought back to the times she and her dad had visited her mother on a dig. There had been a few times that her mom had let her excavate a few pieces. "Not much. I know you use a lot of dental tools and brushes."

Dr. Dodge shook his head. "Well, you can't be any worse than some of the ham-handed workers we've hired out here. They've got no respect for the antiquities archeologists have been taking out of the ground here."

"It's not a lack of respect," Hossam disagreed. "It's just that to most people this is low-paying manual labor. And if a few pieces of pottery are broken, it means little to them. Those pieces may be priceless, but those people also know they'll never own them."

"Recovering those artifacts isn't just about the money," Dr. Dodge argued. "It's for the education we can receive about those ancient civilizations from those recovered pieces."

"Yes, and I know you speak from your heart, my good friend. But these people know what they need. Work that they may fill their bellies and care for their children. Learning of the past is nothing to most of them. It won't change their lives."

Dr. Dodge sighed and rubbed his face with a palm. "I know. It's hard to get someone else to understand the love you have for this kind of work. They either get it or they don't."

Now, there's a quotable quote, Sabrina told herself, making a mental note.

"Let's drink one last cup of that wretched coffee you're so fond of, and I'll be on my way," the professor said.

"What about me?" Sabrina asked.

"The coffee is really terrible," Dr. Dodge warned.

"I'll pass on the coffee. I want to know about the job."

"A job with long hours, terrible living conditions, frustrations every day, back-breaking labor, and no pay?" The professor laughed good-naturedly. "My dear girl, how could I refuse you?"

"Oh, and have you found someone new to use and abuse?"

Sabrina knew that voice at once. She turned slowly and saw her mother standing just outside the office doorway. Dr. Dodge made the introductions and Sabrina shook hands with her mom, not believing how young she looked. She was blond like Sabrina, and only a handful of years older. Her fedora was canted at a rakish angle.

"Hossam's coffee is Turkish," her mom said. "It's dark and sweet, and has enough caffeine to keep an army awake for a month. If you don't think you're up for that, I'll stand you to a glass of iced tea."

"Sure," Sabrina responded numbly. She followed her mom out of the warehouse.

Chapter 10

"I'm sorry you're not more comfortable, Bri."

"It's okay. You weren't exactly expecting company." Sabrina sat in the back of the ancient Willis jeep Dr. Dodge drove through Luxor. The crate containing the generator took up most of the available space. A few more boxes of supplies her mother had gone to the marketplace to get were stacked around her, tied in place with cargo ropes. The ropes were necessary because the roads were bumpy and terrible.

The city went by in a blur, filled mostly with alabaster buildings and homes. Over on the west bank of the Nile River, she saw tall, looming mountains of sand and rock. Living got very hard only a short distance from the river.

Children ran and played in the streets, and clothing still hung out on lines in the residential areas. Downtown Luxor and the waterfront were more civilized, filled with towering hotels and business offices. Pushcart peddlers hawked goods from food to jewelry to souvenir pieces of rare artifacts on street corners.

"This place is so much bigger than I thought," Sabrina said.

"Luxor?" Dr. Dodge veered away from a trio of camels carrying cargo. "It's got a great history."

"The city is built on the ruins of Thebes," Sabrina's mom said. "Gold and slaves built the city, owned by the warrior pharaohs of the Eighteenth Dynasty. Between the years of 1570 and 1090 B.C., it's believed that over a million people lived in Thebes. It was the center of administration and religion."

Dr. Dodge turned again onto another road, heading steadily west now. The mountains lay in the background, still not seeming to get any closer. "That lasted until about 500 B.C. Then invaders sacked the city and took everything they could pack out. The survivors stayed, though. Fertile land, as you can see, is hard to find in this part of Egypt. If the Nile suddenly dried up, so would all the cities."

Sabrina stared at all the beauty around her. No way would she trade the mall for something like this, but it was good to see.

"The people built their homes over the surviving monuments that weren't destroyed by the invaders," her mom said, taking up the story. "Twenty-five hundred years of crammed-together living buried a lot of the tombs under tons of rubble and desert sand. It wasn't until Napoleon sent expeditionary teams into the city and discovered the ruins that the rest of the world got interested in what had happened here."

"The mummies," Sabrina said.

Her mom laughed. "The mummies were a big part of it. But you've got to remember this was one of the birthplaces of civilization. Historians knew there was a lot to learn here."

Seizing the opportunity, Sabrina asked, "So why did you come here?"

Her mom waved at the mountains, the river, the sugarcane fields flanked by palm trees, and the ancient buildings and monuments around them. "How could I not?"

Less than an hour later Dr. Dodge halted the jeep at the main camp near the dig site. They were deep into the mountainous Valley of the Kings now, surrounded on all sides by high, windblown ridges. Frequent dust storms in the area made them put wet handkerchiefs over their mouths and noses.

"So what's the difference between the West Bank and the East Bank?" Sabrina hopped out of the jeep and took up one of the boxes of supplies. Salem walked at her side, obviously not happy about the turn of events. "I mean, other than the obvious compass differences."

The campsite came alive around them as the other members of the archeological party abandoned whatever they'd been working on and came over to help with the supplies. More than a dozen tents, some of them patched and listing badly in the wind, sat staked down in front of a tall foothill that offered little defense from the restless wind and ever-moving sand.

"Most people have always lived along the East Bank," her mom answered. "The pharaohs during the Eighteenth and Nineteenth Dynasties chose to place their tombs on this side of the Nile because this area is small and enclosed by steep cliffs. It makes it easier to defend."

"Ah, a new student comes to our little clan." A huge man with freckles, red hair, and glasses joined Sabrina and her mom. "Welcome. I'm Wayne."

"Not just Wayne," Sabrina's mom said. "Professor Wayne Means, one of the foremost authorities in all things Egyptian in the world. Wayne, meet Bri Kinkle."

"Charmed," the big man rumbled, taking Sabrina's hand and patting it. "I hope you enjoy your stay." He walked to the back of the jeep and hauled the generator out by himself.

"Big guy," Sabrina commented, watching the amazing feat of strength.

"Intelligent guy," her mom replied. "I'm learning a lot from him about hieroglyphics. He's very patient because I'm a slow learner."

"I can't believe that, you're so—" Sabrina caught herself. "You seem so intelligent."

"Probably by most standards I am," her mom

said, leading the way to a cave built into the wall behind the tents. Crates and shelves of foodstuffs, supplies, and equipment filled the small cave. "But not around these guys. It makes me feel intimidated some days."

"Really?" *Wow, Mom has always seemed so together I can't imagine her ever being worried about anything she did.*

"Oh, yeah, these guys are the very best." She put her box down on a small table and began sorting the goods onto the shelves.

"And you're all out here to find Menkhotep's tomb." Sabrina handed the stuff in her box to her mom as other people carried more boxes in.

"If the curse doesn't get us first." Her mom smiled. Her voice echoed in the sudden quiet inside the cave. "Well, that was spooky."

"What is the curse?" Sabrina asked.

"Our studies have revealed that Menkhotep wasn't a ruler," her mom informed her. "We think Menkhotep was an adviser to Rameses I, the founder of the Nineteenth Dynasty. They met in the military and remained friends. What do you know about Rameses?"

"Not enough to take Rameses for five hundred, Alex," Sabrina answered.

"Jeopardy!" her mom said. "I do miss *Jeopardy!* Where did you say you were going to school?"

"Westbridge. It's small. You probably haven't even heard of it. I'm going to be starting the university later this year."

Sabrina's mom picked up another box and started

emptying it, rapidly filling the shelves. "Rameses I wasn't of royal blood, which was kind of unusual for starters. His father was Seti, a military commander from Avaris, a city in the eastern delta region. And he was only pharaoh for one year."

"One year?"

"Yes. But it was a really productive year. He rose in rank in the military, so he learned how to get things done. He conducted military engagements in Asia, reopened the turquoise mines in Sinai, and started building in Buhen. His son was Seti I."

I hope there isn't a test at the end of this, Sabrina thought. Still, it was interesting hearing her mother talk about the subject because she clearly cared about it.

"Seti I started restoring the temples," her mom continued. "He had the Osierion built, which is one of the more famous structures in this area, and he kept up the Asian wars, which enhanced Thebes' position at the time. We believe Menkhotep advised him during those years, but Seti I's son, Rameses II, didn't appear quite so taken with his grandfather's friend after he came to the throne. Our research indicates that Rameses II, later called the Great, banned Menkhotep from the city and decreed that the name be stricken from the records."

"Only they didn't completely do the job."

"No," her mom said. "Rameses the Great's mummy was found in the Deir el-Bahari cache in 1881 and things were missing. Tomb raiders have been a problem since the tombs first started getting built. Only a handful of years ago, Dr. Dodge found a personal record that he believes was taken with some of the articles robbed from Rameses the Great. They mentioned Menkhotep, but the references are vague. However, it was enough to know that Menkhotep had been an adviser to the court since Rameses I."

"If Menkhotep was Rameses the Great's army buddy, he'd have had to be getting pretty old by then."

"Yes, but evidently Rameses the Great still considered him a threat. Shortly after the Battle of Kadesh in 1275 B.C., Rameses II ordered Menkhotep's execution. In the document Dr. Dodge translated, references were made to a tomb located in the East Valley. Only five tombs are in the West Valley, and all of them are Eighteenth Dynasty pharaohs. Anyway, it was during the execution that the curse was made."

"What was the curse?"

Her mom shrugged. "The usual. That if Menkhotep was able to rise from the grave, everyone who'd taken part in the execution, including the children of those men, would be put to death in the most horrible ways that could be imagined."

Sabrina swallowed hard. Images of the mummy clawing its way up from a sarcophagus filled her mind. "You don't seem too worried about it."

"Magic, superstition, and mumbo-jumbo," her mother declared. "They're interesting pieces of human culture, but really—who's going to believe that?"

* * *

Nightfall came quickly over the desert, and with it came an unexpected chill. Sabrina sat with the others near the main campfire, trying to sort out all the people who were with the archeological party. The problem was they all kept moving, off doing their own things, then rejoining the group around the main campfire to take part in a dozen conversations at once.

Her own lack of experience set Sabrina apart from the others. She couldn't hold her own in the conversations. Feeling a little dispirited, she went off by herself, draped in a light blanket to knock off the wind. The heat from the campfire felt good against her face.

Salem poked his head up from the blanket between her arms. "We should be getting back."

"Not yet." Sabrina watched Dr. Means as he approached the seated group with an acoustic guitar in his hand. The archeological group burst out into immediate applause.

"I thought to regale you with yet another of my feeble attempts at music. I hadn't known you all were so bored that you'd think this a welcome relief." Dr. Means sat on one of the spread blankets around the campfire and tuned the guitar. Then, to Sabrina's astonishment, the professor started belting out Lynard Skynard hits, starting with "Sweet Home Alabama."

"You're spending too much time here," Salem objected. "You've got what you need. Your mom just loves this kind of work. You can see that in her."

Sabrina had to admit that was true. "I'm not ready to go yet."

"Why?" The cat's yellow eyes were big. "Have you seen that tent we're going to be sleeping in? You'd find it in the dictionary under the word *hovel.*"

"My mom sleeps there."

"Your mom likes this kind of work. That's what I'm trying to tell you. My sensibilities are more refined."

"You've got the world's biggest sandbox here, and you're a cat," Sabrina told him. "How can you not be happy here?"

"We've been here most of the day," Salem complained. "Trekked across the desert—"

"I did the trekking part."

"True, but I had to endure the heat. Then we nearly had our brains bounced out during the jeep ride to this place. To top it all off, these people don't even believe in mummy curses. They're sitting on a potential powder keg and they don't even know it."

"That's all the more reason to stay."

The crowd gathered around Dr. Means sang along with the chorus as he worked the guitar strings. Sabrina grinned in delight.

"If we get back late . . ." Salem warned.

"This is time travel, remember? I'll just pop us back in a minute or two after we left."

"Time travel isn't as easy as baking a cake," Salem told her, "no matter how easy *The Discovery of Magic* made it sound. There are plenty of witches who went back in time and never returned."

"Maybe they didn't want to."

Salem pushed himself up out of the blankets, cocking his ears. "Besides the whole mummy's curse thing, bad sleeping arrangements, a limited food supply, and the heat, there are other problems with staying here."

"Like what?"

"Like them."

One of the men on the archeological dig zigzagged between the tents, running for all he was worth. "Hey!" he yelled. "The bandits are back! Someone get Dr. Dodge!"

Chapter 11

In moments Sabrina stood with the whole group at the mouth of the box canyon where the archeologists had set up camp. Dr. Dodge stood in front of them, facing the dark men on horseback who came up from the sunlit western sky.

Sabrina thought there might be as many as twenty riders, all of them dressed in black robes and capes like desert nomads. But their clothing and saddles were old and worn. They carried curved swords, rifles, and pistols.

Several of the men in the archeologists' camp, including Dr. Means, held rifles.

Salem curled up more tightly in Sabrina's arms and trembled slightly. "The first time somebody yells, 'Slap leather!' you better be moving."

"It's not going to come to that," Sabrina said, but she wasn't as sure as she tried to sound.

"Dr. Dodge," the lead rider called out. He raised the oil torch he held high into the air so his cruel features could be seen.

"I'm here, Subeih," Dr. Dodge called back.

Subeih raked his harsh gaze over the assembled archeologists. "You were warned about your activities here. You're disturbing things that are better left alone. Now a price has been paid."

"What are you talking about?"

The bandit chief spoke briefly, then one of the riders of his group started forward. Everyone from the archeological camp tensed. When the rider got to the edge of the circle of light of the camp, he pulled his cowl back to reveal ancient and withered features.

"Man," Salem whispered, "that has got to be the oldest guy I've ever seen. He looks like a poster child for I-can't-wait-to-be-a-mummy."

"I'm talking about this, Dr. Dodge. The result of the curse. This is my nephew, Abdel. He is seventeen. Last night I had him watching your camp. Before dawn this morning he was attacked and left for dead. His youth was stripped from him by Menkhotep, leaving only the old man you see before you."

The archeologists started talking at once. Some of them sounded angry and others sounded confused.

The hair on Salem's back rose. "Some kind of

magic is involved in this. You can smell it all over that guy."

Sabrina couldn't, but she didn't doubt her pet. It made her feel creepy.

"I thought you said the curse would only be in effect if we opened the tomb," Dr. Dodge said. "We haven't opened the tomb, or even found it yet."

"Perhaps you are closer than you think." Subeih gestured to the withered man, who covered his face with his cowl again and rode back to join the others.

"Why should I believe you?" Dr. Dodge asked. "For all I know, you're merely passing an old man off as your nephew to scare us."

"With everything you know," Subeih said, "you should already be scared. It has been years since Menkhotep has taken the youth from any man among my group. Now you and your people stir up the past and draw Menkhotep back here."

"I thought Menkhotep was in the grave."

"You think Menkhotep is no threat to you or your people," Subeih said. "You are wrong on both counts. The mummy walks among the living again and has for years. The foul creature has not gotten all its powers back, or it would have already wreaked its vengeance on my tribe. We are descended from the men who executed Menkhotep at Rameses the Great's order."

"Do you know where the tomb is?" Dr. Dodge asked.

"No. Those of us who knew back in those days

buried Menkhotep's mummy, then rode away from our people. None who have lived within my tribe have ever known the location."

"Then you don't know if we're close or not."

Subeih lowered his torch. "You are a fool. Why else would the mummy be stalking your camp?" He jerked his head back, starting his riders back along the way they had come.

"Did your nephew see Menkhotep?" the professor asked.

"Abdel saw a monstrosity," Subeih said. "A thing of nightmare that stole his youth. He barely escaped with his life."

"How can you believe that?" Dr. Dodge demanded. "You're an educated man."

"And you are a blind man walking to his doom. I give you this last warning, Dr. Dodge, because I am willing to stay my hand for a short time more only. But what you will unleash in your greed will only hurt you and those close to you. Either by the mummy's hand—or mine!" The bandit leader threw his torch on the ground. It flickered for a moment, fighting the sand and the wind, then sputtered and went out.

Sabrina listened to the horses' hooves thudding against the hills, but after only a moment, that sound was gone, leaving only the whistling wind.

"Do you believe in the curse?" Sabrina asked her companion.

Dr. Cordwainer Mellon paused for a moment and looked at her. He was a gray scarecrow of a man in ill-fitting clothing that was years past its prime. A week's worth of stubble dotted his sallow cheeks. Sabrina figured he might be seventy years old, but he worked hard.

Dr. Mellon wiped his mouth with a grimy sleeve. "Nah. Curses are just something those trinket dealers scattered across the Valley of the Kings invented thousands of years ago to sell charms to the explorers who came out here with enough gumption and know-how to get into these tombs." He stepped on his shovel gently, driving the blade into the hard ground.

"You saw Subeih's nephew last night." Sabrina concentrated on working loose the big stone in the side of the excavation pit where they'd been working all day. Dr. Dodge had divided them into groups that morning, and Sabrina had been disappointed when she hadn't been assigned with her mom.

It was late afternoon now, and the sun was sinking in the purple skies to the west. The mountains rising around them made her feel the excavation pit was even deeper than it was.

"I saw who that bandit said was his nephew." Dr. Mellon scattered the sand over a wire-mesh screen over a box. A few dirt clods and rocks stayed on the screen while the sand sifted through. The old professor knelt and went through the clods and rocks with a keen, decisive eye. "I was surprised a guy that old could still sit on a horse."

Taking a handkerchief from her pocket, Sabrina mopped at the back of her neck. It didn't help much because the perspiration and sand coated her.

Thankfully the camp had an adequate water supply at this time of year, feeding from a natural cistern on top of the foothill where the cave was so they could have showers. At least until the water turned foul or dried up. She looked forward to a shower.

Dr. Mellon started laughing. "Mummies walking. Stealing a man's youth. What superstitious twaddle. I'm telling you, the only reason these people start stories like that is to sell charms. They started selling them to the French, and they've been selling them to everyone else who's come here since. Me, I've never bought a single one. I won't, either."

"Subeih wasn't selling charms last night," Sabrina disagreed. "It sounded like he was really trying to warn us."

"Sure. And let me tell you what *his* game is." Finished sorting through the rocks and dirt clods, Dr. Mellon stood and picked up the shovel again. "Men like Subeih have black market dealers who arrange transportation of relics that collectors pay top dollar for. He doesn't want to fight us because he knows Dr. Dodge will. He's fought men like Subeih before. But if that old bandit can run off the dig team and he can locate that tomb, he stands to make a lot of money. That's what he's after."

I don't think so. Sabrina still remembered how Salem had told her he could smell magic. She wished the cat was there now, watching over her back, but Salem had remained back at camp, pouting because she hadn't gone home last night.

She and her mother had talked last night, but her mom had been too into the whole tomb theory thing. She'd been too tired to keep her eyes open, either, and thought she'd gone to sleep in the middle of their conversation. That morning had been all hustle and bustle, with no time out for social amenities.

Maybe I should be going home, Sabrina thought as she sat on the big rock. Someone would check the rock over later and make sure nothing was inside. So far they'd found a few things in this location, mainly broken pottery that suggested the area had been used as a campsite upon occasion.

But with the time travel spell working, she knew she had time to spend. And the whole mystery of the lost tomb and the mummy captivated her. Plus, it was really nice to spend time with her mom, even though her mom wasn't her mom yet and didn't realize she was her mom.

That part was totally weird.

"I'm going back to the jeep for a drink of water," Dr. Mellon said. "Would you like anything?"

"No, thanks. I'm fine." Sabrina picked up a small trowel that she'd been using and dug at the hole the big rock had left. Her back, shoulders, and legs hurt from all the digging. She scooped dirt out of the hole, then heard a metallic scrape.

Curious, she took the flashlight from the toolkit she'd been given and shined it into the hole. White rock glinted at the back of the hole, not quite eighteen inches deep. The rock was suspiciously flat-sided, as if it had been quarried.

Reaching inside, she traced two of the edges of the stone block. She also felt the crevice between it and the next block. Excited, knowing that whatever she'd found was definitely man-made, she used the trowel to enlarge the hole where the rock had been.

The packed sand seemed to fall from the hole, spreading across her knees. Excitement and curiosity pushed away the tiredness. In minutes she'd opened a hole large enough to wedge her body into.

There wasn't just one stone block at the back of the hole; there was a wall of them.

Sabrina raised her voice. "Dr. Mellon."

The professor didn't answer back.

Intent on her discovery, Sabrina pushed into the hole. She slid her fingers into the space between the blocks. They were set at an incline that followed the contour of the excavation pit. When she pulled on the block, it moved ever so slightly.

"Dr. Mellon."

For a moment, Sabrina thought she'd go after the old professor and tell him what she'd found. But she couldn't. She thought the stone block was ready to come out, and she wanted to be the first to move it. She pushed her way into the hole and put her weight against it. The block moved again, but still didn't come free.

She pointed and said,

Earth below, sky above,
Give these rocks a mighty shove.

Too late she realized she should have found something to rhyme with the word pull. Without warning, the rock wall she'd uncovered exploded inward out from under her. She fell into the waiting darkness.

Chapter 12

Don't scream, don't scream, Sabrina told herself as she tried not to panic. She rolled twice, then landed hard against an unyielding surface. Screaming always draws the yucky things, the slimy things, the muck-encrusted things.

She flailed in the darkness, spotting the hole above her. *I need to be home with Harvey; that's where I really should be.* The sticky strands of a spider's web caressed her neck. *Gross!* She expected to feel the creepy-crawl of eight legs moving over her at any time.

Concentrating, she pointed up a flashlight, promising herself if she spotted any spiders she was going to zap them a million miles away. She turned the beam on, splashing the sides of the underground passageway with bright light.

"Hey, you okay down there?"

Glancing up, Sabrina spotted Dr. Mellon framed in the opening she'd dug. "I think so."

The first smile she'd ever seen lit up the old professor's face. "Good. Because I think you're going to be a hero, little lady."

"I don't feel like much of a hero," Sabrina griped a little later. "Not after getting chewed out by Dr. Dodge."

"Dr. Dodge was just worried about you," her mom said. "He's got rules you're supposed to operate by. You could have been badly hurt. You got lucky."

Sabrina stood beside her mom around the excavation pit she and Dr. Mellon had been working. Dr. Dodge and three other men, including Dr. Means, worked at shoring up the sides of the tunnel Sabrina had discovered. They put in new timbers to support the walls. The rest of the crew stood around anxiously. Two trucks with gasoline-powered generators parked nearby provided electricity for the string of lights hung around the area.

Sabrina watched her mom, enjoying the glow on her face. *This really is what she lives for.*

Dr. Dodge called for a flash, then crept a little farther into the tunnel.

"Do you think this really is the way into Menkhotep's tomb?" Sabrina asked.

Her mom shrugged, her eyes never leaving the excavation pit. "I couldn't say for sure, but maybe. We knew it had to be at one of the four excavation sites. Menkhotep wasn't royalty, but the tomb was located within the Nineteenth Dynasty grounds, according to the documents Dr. Dodge found."

Sabrina waited breathlessly. She watched the lights move around in the excavation pit. A muffled thump sounded, then a gush of dust billowed from the tunnel mouth.

Dr. Dodge emerged a couple moments later, coughing his head off, his face all covered in dust. "Okay, people, this is it. We have found Menkhotep's tomb."

A loud cheer went up from the dig crew, and Sabrina joined in immediately. *I found it. I really found it!*

"Did you sleep well?"

Sabrina took a seat beside her mom at one of the folding tables where the dig crew lunched. Breakfast was generally the only meal most of the team got together for. Morning was still a pale promise in the east, partially hidden behind an acid-yellow cloud layer created by dust storms. "Yes."

Despite the excitement that ran rampant through the archeological camp, Dr. Dodge ordered everyone back to their quarters for the evening except two men who offered to stand guard over the tomb area. Surprisingly, even after Subeih's appearance that night, no one got overly worried about the mummy's curse.

Sabrina, however, did experience some anxiety, but it hadn't kept fatigue from claiming her for six hours of sleep. Archeology was even less restful than high school. She looked at her mom, noticing the dark circles under her eyes. "You don't look like you got much rest."

When she'd fallen asleep, her mom had still been awake, reading through the translation Dr. Dodge had made on the Menkhotep document by lantern light.

Her mom stifled a yawn with a quick hand. "Not much," she agreed.

"If I could get your attention, people." Dr. Dodge stood at the head of one of the other breakfast tables. The only thing that looked fresh about him was his clothes, but excitement filled him. He waited till everyone grew quiet. "As you can see, I've clearly spared no expense at breakfast this morning."

Polite laughter, a smattering of applause, and a couple heartfelt cheers followed his announcement.

The breakfast selection was better, Sabrina had to admit. Besides cereals, eggs, rashers of bacon, and hash browns, there was also an abundance of fresh fruit sliced and ready to eat. Fortunately the weather seemed inclined to be agreeable, and there weren't any sudden dust storms to crust it all over if it wasn't eaten hand-to-mouth.

"This is a big day for us," Dr. Dodge went on. "We'll start the framing work on the tomb today, shoring up the passageway that Miss Kinkle discovered."

Another cheer went up, followed by enthusiastic applause.

"See?" her mom whispered, adding into the applause. "You are a hero."

Sabrina's cheeks burned with embarrassment, but

she felt good, too. The only real thing worrying her was Salem's absence. As far as she knew, the cat had never made it in last night.

A sudden *whap-whap-whapping* noise filled the air. Everyone looked up, spotting the helicopter with Egyptian government markings as it flew in from Luxor. Conversation died as the dig team watched the aircraft settle outside the camp.

Uh-oh, Sabrina thought, watching how tense the members of the archeological crew got, *this can't be good.*

Three men in business suits crossed the sand to the camp. The man in front was small and dark with a shaved head and a full salt-and-pepper beard. "Dr. Edmund Dodge," he called out in accented English.

"That's me," Dr. Dodge said.

The man crossed to the professor and extended a letter. "These are cease-and-desist orders from the Egyptian government, sir. You and your people have to stop the excavation you are currently on till the matter can be reviewed."

The crew started arguing with the man at once, their voices getting louder and louder. Dr. Dodge opened the envelope he'd been given and reviewed the contents. "All right," the professor roared. "Enough!"

The dig crew quieted.

"It's a setback," Dr. Dodge said, facing his team. "We've had them before. But this will not be a show-stopper." He turned back to the government repre-sentative. "Tell your people I'll be talking to them."

The mood over the camp darkened immediately.

They watched in silence as the men returned to the helicopter and took off.

"This is so unfair," Sabrina's mom said.

The teenage witch nodded. She felt totally bummed even though she knew this was going to happen. It had all been detailed in her mom's journal. "Don't worry. I don't think this is going to last long."

"It's not," Dr. Dodge asserted. "There's a young man in the American Consulate I had the opportunity to meet a few months back when I was arranging for this dig. He's very good at these things. His name is—"

"You mean Edward Spellman?" asked Sabrina's mom. At Dr. Dodge's and Sabrina's surprised looks, she said somewhat offhandedly, "Oh, we've met before." Sabrina stared at her mother. Her cheeks were flushed!

"Spellman. Edward Spellman." Sabrina's dad offered his hand to Dr. Dodge. Despite the heat, he wore a black Italian suit that was perfectly tailored. His dark hair moved slightly in the breeze, and he didn't look any different than Sabrina remembered him. "I'm with the American Consulate."

"I'm glad you could come, Ted," Dr. Dodge replied. He quickly made the introductions to the handful of archeologists who'd accompanied him down to meet Edward.

Sabrina shook her own father's hand as if she were just meeting him. *This is really too weird,* she couldn't help thinking. *I'm actually meeting my dad before he meets me.*

But that was nothing as weird as seeing the sparks that passed between her mom and her dad when they shook hands. In spite of the fact that her mom was grimed over from working on some of the artifacts the team had recovered so far, her dad took longer holding her hand than anyone else's.

"It's great to see you again," he said.

"Likewise," her mom replied, making no move to take her hand from his. She smiled. "I just hope you're as good as you look."

Mom! Sabrina thought, embarrassed to see her mom flirting like—like—*Like a girl not much older than I am,* the teenage witch realized.

Her dad smiled, oozing charm. "Oh, I am."

Sabrina didn't know which of them was worse.

Dr. Dodge, though, hurried on through the introductions, taking Edward by the elbow and guiding him toward the camp. They sat at the breakfast tables.

"I came as quickly as I could," her dad said as Dr. Dodge passed coffee around in paper cups. It was the afternoon of the same day the dig had been ordered to cease and desist. "I've been quite interested in your work."

Sabrina didn't know if that was true or not, but her dad made it sound true.

"We just found the entrance to Menkhotep's tomb last night," Dr. Dodge said.

"So I heard," Edward commented. "The news was all over the consulate this morning. As was the fact that the Egyptian government was shutting you down."

"Why?" the professor asked.

"There is a small group with a large impact on the Egyptian government," Edward said. "They want to send in their own crews to do the excavation."

"That's not fair," Sabrina's mom said. "We've put in time finding this tomb. Even before we broke ground, Dr. Dodge had put in months finding the document that led us here and doing the translation."

"I'm very aware of that," Edward said, turning his full attention to Sabrina's mom. "I find it very unfair, too. That's why I'm here now."

"Are you going to be able to help us?" Dr. Means rumbled from the other end of the table.

"If I couldn't help you," Edward said confidently, "I wouldn't have come here. As it is, I've already implemented measures that should take the pressure off."

"How?" Sabrina's mom asked. "What about this lobbying group you're talking about?"

"Miss," Edward said, with a twinkle in his eyes, "that lobbying group may have a big impact on the Egyptian government, but I can assure you they in no way have as much influence as the American government. And, despite the support back home, I've also managed to round up a rather influential backer locally, too. I think we're going to be just fine."

"I'll be interested to see how much of that you can really do," Sabrina's mom said.

Edward grinned. "I do love a challenge. If I'm

right, let's say you owe me dinner one night when you're free."

"Do you enjoy eating out of a tin plate, Mr. Spellman?" Sabrina's mom asked.

"Considering the company, I don't think I'll find that too much of a hardship."

Sabrina saw spots of color appear in her mom's cheeks. The teenage witch couldn't keep from smiling. *This is so romantic.*

Unbelievably, her mom pushed up from the table. "I'll look forward to hearing from you." She turned and walked away, then stopped. "By the way, Mr. Spellman, what happens if you're wrong?"

"Why," he said easily, "I owe you dinner, of course. Do you mind eating by candlelight?"

Sabrina's mom smiled and walked away without comment. The teenage witch hurried after her. *How were they going to get together if her mom kept walking away?*

"What are you doing?" Sabrina asked when she caught up to her mom in their tent. "He's a total hottie."

Her mom raised her eyebrows. "A hottie?"

Okay, so they don't have that term yet, Sabrina thought. "You know what I mean."

"If you mean that he's a total babe," her mom said, "I totally agree."

"Aren't you interested?"

"Yes," her mom replied, picking up the notes she'd made last night and organizing them. "But someone like Mr. Edward Spellman likes a challenge. He said so himself."

"But this way he doesn't even know if you're interested in him." Sabrina felt momentary panic. Salem had warned her of the dangers of time-traveling into her own past. What if her being there affected the meeting between her parents? What if they decided they really didn't like each other?

"You don't have to worry about that," her mom replied. "I think he's confident every woman he meets is interested in him."

"But what if you're wrong?"

"Bri," her mom said, "first and foremost, I'm an archeologist, not a boy-crazy teenager. I'm here to work a dig site, not chase after a date."

"But dating is good."

"There's a time and place. Right now I'm more interested in getting that tomb open than in having Edward Spellman give me the time of day." She gathered the materials she was working with and headed out of the tent.

Sabrina watched her go, feeling more nervous than ever. Her mom not all that interested in her dad? That wasn't good. She started getting worried.

"So, starting to get a little more aware of the dangers of traveling into your own past?" a familiar voice asked.

Glancing back at her unmade sleeping cot, Sabrina spotted Salem lying in the sheets. "Where have you been?"

"Scouting the countryside," the cat replied.

"Since you were so caught up in digging, I didn't think you'd miss me."

"I did. I was getting worried."

"Not to fear. I always land on my feet."

"Did you find out anything interesting?" Sabrina stripped the bedclothes from the cot and started making it.

Salem yowled in surprise and landed on his side on the floor of the tent with a smack. "As a matter of fact, I found out that the local bandit chief, Subeih, has camped out not far from here. He's a very cagey guy, and I haven't quite figured out what his game is."

"What about the suddenly-old nephew?"

"Oh, that's real. There was another one last night who lost his youth."

A chill passed through Sabrina. "Did you see the mummy?"

"No, but I have a feeling it's out there." Salem blinked at her. "Are you ready to go home yet?"

Sabrina shook her head. "They don't even believe in the mummy or the curse. I can't just leave them."

"This has already happened, Sabrina. If you involve yourself in it too much, you could end up affecting that, too."

"Maybe I already have. I was the one who found the tomb."

Salem's eyes rounded. "Did your mother's journal mention that?"

"No. Only that a young college student found it."

"Hmmmm," the cat said. "You may have already affected things here."

"So we'll need to stay and make sure everything turns out all right, right?" Sabrina finished making the cot.

"I'd suggest you tell one of your aunts what's going on here."

"Not a plan," Sabrina said. "I don't think they'd understand this at all." She paused. "If things get worse, maybe then."

The cat jumped up onto the cot and curled up. "Maybe you'd like to join me in the chorus of 'I Am My Own Grandpa.' "

Sabrina threw a pillow at him.

A second limousine arrived at the campsite just as evening started to turn the sky dark, draping shadows in from the mountain. Sabrina stood with the rest of the archeological crew and watched as Edward went down to meet it. He reached into the back and helped a woman out.

"Who is this?" Sabrina's mom asked. "His dinner date?"

Dr. Dodge shook his head. "He's been talking about a mysterious benefactor off and on all afternoon. Someone local who added weight to the American effort to get us permission to begin the excavation."

The woman walked with easy grace across the sand, holding firmly on to Edward's arm. She wore a dark blue sheath dress and looked as if she'd just arrived from a cocktail party.

The campsite was lit up by strings of lights powered by the gasoline generators throbbing in the background. Dr. Dodge had held dinner for the new arrival, and the tables were burdened with food.

Edward stepped back into the campsite with the woman on his arm. He had a grin on his face that went from ear to ear.

The woman was dusky-skinned with liquid, magnetic black eyes. She was petite, hardly coming up to Edward's shoulder, but was an exotic beauty. A silver and turquoise headband held her long dark hair back.

"Ladies and gentlemen," Edward said, "may I introduce Miss Cantara Wasef. She'll be joining us for dinner."

Sabrina glanced at her mom, wondering how she was taking the new arrival. Her mom, however, was one of the first to go forward and introduce herself. Sabrina couldn't help noticing the differences in the two women, Cantara in her beautiful cocktail dress and her mom in unflattering khakis.

This isn't good at all, Sabrina thought, watching her mom walk away. *Why didn't Mom's journal mention Cantara Wasef? How could she leave out anyone like this?*

Or was this one of those history-altering changes Salem had been warning her about?

☆

Chapter 13

☆

"I came as quickly as I was able," Cantara Wasef said. Her voice was accented and melodic. She sat to the right of Edward at the campsite's main table. Edward sat at the opposite end of the table from Dr. Dodge. "I knew you would want the news."

"What news?" the professor asked.

"Ted and I have successfully negotiated your case," the exotic woman replied. "You'll have your permission papers by courier the first thing in the morning. Shortly after that, you'll be digging again."

A cheer rose from the dig team, drowning out even the throb of the electrical generators.

"I've got to tell you, Miss Wasef—" Dr. Means said in his deep voice.

"Call me Cantara. All my friends do." The woman dripped charm.

"Wow, what a hottie," Salem purred in Sabrina's ear. He'd just joined her at the table, finally dragging himself from the cot after sleeping all afternoon.

"Be quiet," Sabrina admonished, glancing around quickly to make sure no one had heard the cat. "She's not all that hot." But the woman was, and the teenage witch knew it. She was also aware of how much attention her dad was giving the woman.

Dr. Means smiled. "Fine then. I've got to tell you, Cantara, that I've seen all your movies, and you've never seemed more the heroine than you do right now."

She smiled graciously. "Thank you, Professor."

A movie star? Sabrina thought. She's good looking, rich, and a movie star? She glanced at her mom across the table, who'd been unusually quiet through the meal. *Mom is already giving up. I'm doomed to be unborn.* Her mind raced frantically, trying to find some solution.

"I wasn't aware of your interest in Egyptology or excavations," Dr. Dodge said. "I've been to several fund-raising banquets in Luxor and Cairo, and I've never seen you there. If I had, I know I wouldn't have forgotten."

Cantara laughed melodically. "No. My career is quite high profile. My publicist and agent agree that I must keep my interests to myself as much as possible. Otherwise I would be at the mercy of needy people every hour of the day."

Needy people? Sabrina thought sarcastically. But even though she was offended, none of the others on the dig team seemed to be. They were positively enchanted.

"Why are you so interested in archeology?" Dr. Dodge asked.

"I am from these people," Cantara replied. "My blood is their blood, my culture and history is their culture and history. How could I not be interested in those things? Even during my travels to America and Europe, I've never long forgotten where my roots are. That's why I make my first home here, in these lands."

"What makes this dig so appealing to you?"

"Only that you were denied access to this tomb you have discovered," Cantara said. "When darling Edward called me today and told me of your plight, I couldn't resist helping your cause."

"Actually," Edward said, "Cantara had expressed interest in this dig months ago when the paperwork was first being approved."

Months ago? Sabrina couldn't help wondering how long her dad had known the actress. And why didn't her mother's journal ever mention Cantara Wasef?

"If all goes well," Dr. Dodge said, "we should be opening the tomb in the next few days. Perhaps, if your schedule is light enough, you'd like to be here for that."

"I shall *make* my schedule light enough," Cantara said. "I'd like very much to be here for that."

"I'm afraid accommodations here aren't what you're used to."

"Luxor is not so very far away," the actress said. "There are many fine places to stay there. And I shall eagerly await your call of success when the time comes."

"You could try to go talk to him, you know," Sabrina said.

Her mom looked up from the floor of the tent they shared. An oil lamp hung from the main support pole, illuminating the papers she made notations on. "Who?"

Duh! Sabrina had watched her mom watching her dad who was watching Cantara Wasef all evening until Dr. Dodge called an end to the dinner so everyone could get an early start. "Edward."

"Not interested." Her mom went back to her papers.

"How can you be not interested? You told me earlier today that he was a babe."

"A major babe," her mother corrected. "And I meant it. He's also distracted."

"By the movie star?"

"Did you happen to see anyone else ravishing and beautiful out there?"

"Yes. You."

Her mom turned back to her work. "Thanks for the compliment, but I've got a lot to do here, and I don't need any distractions myself."

"So she's a movie star," Sabrina said. "Don't you think guys fell for Mary Ann, too?"

Her mom's brow wrinkled for a moment. "Oh, you mean on *Gilligan's Island*."

Sabrina nodded.

"I also noticed that Mary Ann ran around in a

crop top and shortie-shorts. Sorry, that's not my style. I'm not some school girl looking for a crush, Bri."

"But he likes you. He really likes you."

"And you know this how?"

Sabrina thought rapidly but couldn't come up with anything convincing. "You can just tell." *That's lame.*

"Look, I really appreciate the support. When I first saw Edward, I thought there might be something there. But with the movie star in the picture, I know I was wrong. And I'd really rather not discuss this anymore. I've got a lot of work to do."

Sabrina wanted to argue, but she knew it was no use. When her mom used that tone of voice, there was no changing her mind. She knew from experience. At least, she *would* know from experience.

If I'm ever born.

It didn't help that Salem had managed to disappear again. Morosely, she climbed into her cot, still bone-tired from all the activity of the past three days. As she drifted off to sleep, she couldn't help wondering if she would realize when she started to disappear.

The dig went well over the next three days. There wasn't much for Sabrina to do except help clean some of the items they removed from the sand and dirt. She watched Dr. Dodge and the excavation crew laboriously remove bucket after bucket of sand, carrying it off and spreading it a hundred yards from the excavation pit.

The tunnel Sabrina had found grew steadily

longer, shored up by cedar timbers the professor had trucked in for that purpose. Meals were eaten by the pit, and conversations stayed at fever-pitch speculation.

Her mom stayed busy cataloging and sketching all the items that were recovered. There wasn't much, but no one was surprised by that. Menkhotep had been executed, not one of the pharaoh's favorites. Dr. Dodge remained hopeful that more than gold or artifacts would be recovered. Menkhotep was reputed to be a chronicler and a scholar, investing time in arcane arts.

Her dad stayed around the dig site as well. He'd cleared his schedule, saying he'd taken more than a casual interest in what was going on.

Dr. Dodge worked the excavation crew well after dark, trying desperately to break through to the tomb's interior. But the passageway leading into it had collapsed over the centuries, filling with sand, rock, and debris, making the work very slow.

"It's no use," he called out at nearly ten o'clock. "We're not going to break through tonight. We've gone back seventy feet. I don't know how much farther it might be before we reach the tomb. Let's call it a night and save fuel oil in the generators."

He posted six guards around the entrance to the passageway. Sabrina hadn't been the only one who'd felt watchful eyes on her.

"You've been avoiding me."

Seated across from her mother at one of the

smaller folding tables around the campfire, Sabrina looked up and saw her father approaching them.

"Me?" her mom asked.

Her father grinned. "Yes."

"I've been working."

He nodded. "I'll agree with that because I've been watching you. You're a very detail-oriented person."

"It's a good thing to be in this field," her mom said.

"You also like what you do," her dad said.

"It's the nature of the work," her mom replied. "You love it or you hate it. If you hate it, you find something else to do. You often go long periods between rewards for all the time you invest."

"I happen to be a believer in long-term investments, too."

Sabrina's mom raised her eyebrows. "You do? Somehow I didn't get that impression."

"Maybe you haven't gotten to know me well enough. May I join you?"

Sabrina's mom shoved aside a stack of papers. "Sure."

Edward sat. "I also wanted to discuss the matter of the dinner you owe me. I'd like to know when we can set that up."

Sabrina tried not to get caught watching her mom. *Don't blow this, don't blow this!*

"Name a time," her mom replied. "I'd be more than happy to open a couple cans and dump them on a tin plate for you."

"It's not exactly gourmet the way you're making it sound."

"No. And I have to wonder how you'd find time for dinner in your busy schedule."

"I've freed myself up from the consulate for a few days. And I have the option of extending that."

"It's not the consulate I was referring to," Sabrina's mom said.

"You mean Cantara?" Edward looked as if he couldn't believe it. "Why, we're just friends."

"Awfully chummy."

"She's an easy person to get to know."

"I'm not surprised."

Feeling suddenly awkward listening to them, Sabrina stood and said, "If you'll excuse me, I gotta go. Back to the tent. Maybe get some sleep."

"Thank you," her dad said without looking up.

"Sit," her mom ordered. "I was just leaving." She gathered her papers and walked away from the table.

Edward smiled and watched her go. "She is one stubborn woman."

"She's really great after you get to know her," Sabrina offered.

"Oh, I'm sure she is," her father said. "But don't worry about that. I like stubbornness. It's not exactly an endearing trait, but it is an honest one. Have you known her long?"

Sabrina shrugged. "It feels like years."

"I'd like to know more about her."

"Work at it," Sabrina suggested. "You've got her attention."

"I do? I thought that was only rancor in her eyes."

"You just didn't look closely enough." Sabrina

felt really nervous, as if she were standing at the edge of a very high cliff with a cold wind at her back. *What do I say? What do I not say?* "I don't want to be rude, but I've got a really big day tomorrow." *If I haven't been unborn by then.*

"Of course." Her father got up from the table politely until she left, then he sat back down to his lonely meal.

Hurrying across the campsite to the tent she shared with her mother, Sabrina was relieved to see her shadow on the tent walls. She parted the tent flaps and stepped through.

Her mother looked up from the floor, seated in the middle of her papers. "You have something on your mind."

Sabrina took a deep breath. *Calm, you've gotta be calm. You can't act like your whole future depends on this. Or your past.* "I think you're making a mistake where Edward is concerned."

"You do?"

"Yes." *That sounded definite without sounding too pushy, didn't it?*

"Well, if it is, it's my mistake to make, isn't it?"

Ooops. "Sorry. That was my mistake." Sabrina pointed toward the tent flaps. "I'll be going now. Exit stage left." She turned to go.

"Bri, wait."

Sabrina turned back around, feeling really torn in what she was supposed to do or say. Her parents were supposed to be together or she wouldn't exist. Yet, they hadn't stayed together after they'd married. Could she be so selfish as to not want what was best for them?

"Do you really think he's interested?" her mom asked.

"I know he is. He just told me. He likes stubborn women."

Her mom smiled. "I guess I have been a little standoffish."

Sabrina held her forefinger and thumb a fraction of an inch apart. "Maybe a little."

"It's just that it's been so long since I've been around someone like him. I've been out in the field and nowhere near a beautician in months."

"You always said beauty was only skin deep," Sabrina told her, recalling past conversations she'd had with her mom.

"When did I tell you this?" Her mom looked confused.

Sabrina tried to cover her mistake. "That wasn't you? I could have sworn that was you. It sounded a lot like you." She smiled. "You know, even if it wasn't you, it was really good advice."

Her mom's expression lacked conviction.

"Edward is interested in you," Sabrina went on. "And you like what you see. Work with that."

"Maybe you're right."

"I know I'm right."

Her mom reached under her cot and pulled out a battered makeup case. She flipped it open to reveal a nearly depleted store of cosmetics. "Me and old Mother Hubbard."

"Don't worry." Sabrina knelt under her own cot and quickly pointed up a makeup kit that she took out of her backpack. "I've got some stuff we can use." She peeked through the tent flap and found that Dr. Dodge had descended on her dad with notes and graphs. "C'mon, we've gotta hurry before he wanders off."

"I haven't felt this nervous in years."

Sabrina stood behind her mom and looked into the reflection of them in the mirror. "Good. That means something." She'd washed her mother's hair from a canteen, then trimmed it with a pair of magic scissors she'd pointed up. They'd worked quickly, using only a little makeup because her mom looked naturally great without it.

The chance to get her mom ready for a "date" struck Sabrina as insane, but at the same time it was endearing. They'd had other mother-daughter moments in the past, but she knew this one was special, never to be forgotten. And when she got to see her mom again soon, maybe she could even tell her about it.

Provided she didn't get unborn.

"What does it mean?" her mother asked.

"That you care enough to make a good impression," Sabrina said, remembering how she'd always dressed for her dates with Harvey. "That you're making an investment. In yourself as well as him. Feel good about yourself and everything's going to work out fine."

"That's what I've always been afraid of," her mom confided in a quiet voice.

"What?"

"Things not working out."

Sabrina looked at her mom and thought about the divorce her parents had gone through. It hadn't been easy for either of them, or her for that matter. Yet, here she was pushing her mom and dad straight into that again. "I don't blame you," she whispered.

"Do you have someone in your life?" her mom asked.

"Yes." Sabrina smiled, remembering Harvey. She'd only been gone minutes from his life, but he'd been gone days from hers. She missed him and wanted a hug so bad. But if things didn't work out here, she'd never see him again.

"What's his name?"

"Harvey."

Her mom brushed at her hair again. "You like him?"

"More than anyone I've ever been out with."

"How can you know that it's going to work?"

"I don't," Sabrina replied. "We've had our problems." *More so than the average couple,* she admitted to herself.

"Then why try?"

"Because of how I feel when I'm with him. He makes me laugh." She thought about his Career Day paper about the giant alligators in New York's sewers. "And he makes me happy."

"Would you give up," her mom asked, "if you knew it wasn't going to work out in the end? Even if you could have a few months or years of this kind of happiness, would it be better to forget it all now so you don't have to worry about later?"

"No. I'd rather have Harvey for the time I can have him and be happy the way he makes me than never to have known that at all."

"You're sure?"

Sabrina nodded.

"My career is hard on marriages," her mom said. "Too much time apart, and I love what I do."

"You should. You're good at it."

Her mom took a deep breath. "Okay, let's see how this works out. He may take one look and head for the hills."

"I don't think so."

"That's because you're prejudiced. You did my hair." Her mom stood and looked at her a moment, her hands trembling. "Wow, guess I'm more nervous than I thought."

Sabrina smiled at her. "You're going to be okay. I promise." *There's a lot of happiness in those early years of the marriage, Mom. You'll see.*

"Thanks, Bri." Her mom stepped over to her and hugged her tightly.

A lump rose in Sabrina's throat as she hugged her back.

Her mom released her. "Gotta go. Otherwise I'm going to chicken out on you." She turned and went through the tent flaps.

Peering through the tent flaps, Sabrina watched as her dad spotted her mom. Edward turned his attention from Dr. Dodge at once. Sabrina let out a tense breath when her mom and dad talked briefly, then the professor got the hint and excused himself.

Her mom sat at the table across from her dad. Edward adjusted the lantern on the table so it caught them both. He smiled.

Sabrina's stomach rolled. Was this it? Was this the deciding moment when she'd be all right, or was she going to be unborn before she could draw her next breath?

Chapter 14

Everything's good so far. Sabrina let out a tense breath. The last handful of minutes had passed slowly, and she'd felt every thump of her heart inside her chest. But her mom and dad seemed to be talking easily, even laughing every now and then.

A metallic tinkle sounded behind her.

Turning, Sabrina approached her cot. The tinkle sounded again. She stripped the bedclothes from the cot but found nothing. Dropping to her knees, she peered under the bed.

"Uh-oh," Salem said. The cat was curled up in the back corner, wreathed in shadows. Dulled yellow gleamed between his front paws.

"What are you doing?" Sabrina demanded.

"Nothing," the cat answered.

"I have a hard time believing that. You keep having these strange disappearances."

"I wouldn't call them strange."

"What would you call them?" Sabrina lifted the cot up, revealing the small pile of gold and silver coins the cat had been pushing into a leather bag.

"Profitable?"

"What have you got?"

"Money," Salem answered. "And it's mine. I dug up a few little trinkets and managed to sell them to the bandits."

"You've been dealing with the bandits?" Sabrina couldn't believe it. "You've been selling artifacts?"

"Small ones. You wouldn't believe how little they pay for them."

"Salem, that's black marketing."

"I wouldn't call it marketing exactly," the cat argued. "Consider this a little mom-and-pop operation. And there's not enough here to feed both."

Pointing at the coins, Sabrina zapped them into the bag and picked the bag up. "You're not getting these."

Salem started sobbing, reaching a paw for the bag. "You can't take those. They're mine, mineminemine!"

Gunshots echoed outside, interrupting Sabrina's argument. She hurried to the tent flaps and peered out.

Mounted bandits rode through the campsite with blazing weapons. So far none of their bullets had hit anyone, and Sabrina didn't think they were really trying, but the archeologists ran for their lives. Driving their horses with spurs, the bandits galloped through tents, tearing the flimsy structures down with ease.

Dr. Dodge tried to rally some of the men, bawling out orders. Another bandit tied a rope around a fuel can and dragged it through the main campfire. The explosion when the fuel mixture caught fire threw flames for yards in all directions. Tents blazed despite the flame-retardant materials they were made of.

"That," Salem stated at Sabrina's feet, "is our cue to leave."

"No." Sabrina watched as two bandits rode toward her mom and dad. Edward grabbed her mom by the arm and pulled her to safety an instant before the galloping horses crushed the folding table under their hooves.

Her dad pointed at the nearest horse and the animal suddenly crashed into the one next to it. Both went down in heaps, spilling the riders from the saddles.

"These are the bandits you've been trading with?" Sabrina asked. She pointed at one of the horses and caused it to start bucking till it kicked its riders off.

"I don't think there's another bunch of bandits in the area," Salem said. "So yeah. Maybe." He stuck his muzzle through the tent flaps, then drew back immediately. "This environment is definitely not cat-friendly."

"What is their problem?"

"I think it's the fact that a lot of their people are getting ready for the senior citizens' home. When I was last at their camp, there must have been a dozen or more guys that looked like one or both parents were prunes. They've been talking about tearing up the archeology campsite and making everybody go home."

Sabrina's mom got to her feet and shoved Edward away as two more bandits tried to run them down. Moving quickly, she seized a tent pole from a shredded tent and held it in both hands. Sparks flew when she blocked one of the bandits' swords, then she stepped around and slid her hands to the bottom of the tent pole. She swung the pole off her shoulder like a baseball bat, hitting the bandit in the back of the head and knocking him from the horse.

"Yay, Mom!" Sabrina shouted.

"Move!" Salem squalled, shoving a shoulder against her calf.

The thunder of thudding hooves grew louder in Sabrina's ears. She pushed out of the tent just ahead of the bandit on horseback that rode through their tent. The heavy canvas swaddled the horse, causing it to stumble.

Sabrina ran to her mom, who planted one end of the tent pole on the ground and lifted it to meet the other rider making a second pass at her. The tent pole caught the man in the chest, bent double for a moment, then pushed him off into the air.

"The bandits were also talking about dynamiting the tomb to destroy it," Salem said as they dodged over the debris filling the campsite.

"What?" Sabrina felt ready to freak. "Why didn't you mention this earlier?"

"It didn't come up," Salem said.

Sabrina ran for her mom and dad. "They're going to blow up the tomb," she told them.

"You're sure?" her father asked.

"I overheard them talking about it," Sabrina said. "I don't know if they're going to do it tonight or some other time."

"We need to check on that."

Sabrina's mom glanced around quickly. "We'll take a jeep." She ran, taking the lead, dodging behind flaming tents and leaping overturned tables. Instead of following the trail out of the box canyon where the campsite was, she scaled the side of the canyon ten feet up and hauled herself over the edge.

Edward gave Sabrina a boost as Salem easily made the climb. Catching hold of the edge, Sabrina pulled herself up, barely beating her dad. Her mom was already racing down the incline toward the parked camp vehicles. In seconds she was behind the steering wheel and had the engine turning over.

Breathing hard, Sabrina dropped into the passenger seat while her dad clambered up into the back. Like a shot, Salem vaulted into Sabrina's lap.

"Belt up," her mom ordered. Then she put her foot down on the accelerator. All four wheels threw sand and rock out as the vehicle sped toward the excavation site.

Sabrina watched her mom driving in total disbelief. *And this is the woman I used to have to heckle to get me to school on time?* The teenage witch hung on to the seat belts as the jeep lurched and jerked across the uneven terrain. For the first time, she noticed the full moon hanging above the mountains.

"That was a nice move with the tent pole back there!" Edward shouted above the roar of the engine. He hung on to the roll bar, his dusty jacket flapping around him.

"Thanks," Sabrina's mom said. "Just a couple moves I picked up in a martial arts class I took."

"You took martial arts?" Sabrina asked in surprise. "I never knew that."

"We haven't gotten to know each other very well," her mom replied.

No, I guess we haven't. Sabrina promised to make up for lost time when she got the chance. *Parents are interesting. Who knew?*

The jeep skidded to a stop only a few feet from the excavation pit, throwing a thick cloud of sand and dust into it. Sabrina's mom shut off the engine, dropped the keys to the floor, and heaved herself out of the vehicle.

Two black-clad bandits stood up from the shadows suddenly. Swords gleamed in their fists. At their feet were the unconscious bodies of the guards Dr. Dodge had left behind.

Sabrina's mom stopped short but didn't give any indication of backing away.

From the corner of her eye, Sabrina saw her dad point his forefinger at the bandits. Almost immediately, the two men dropped in their tracks without a sound.

"How did you do that?" Sabrina's mom demanded.

Edward opened his hand, revealing the pistol Sabrina knew hadn't been there earlier. Her dad had used witchcraft, then pointed up a weapon. "Tranquilizer pistol. Very effective and nonlethal. The consulate prefers us to be able to protect ourselves without serious political repercussions." He gestured toward the open pit. "Shall we?"

Sabrina couldn't help grinning as she picked Salem up. "Aren't they great?" she whispered proudly.

"Yeah, yeah, yeah," the cat said. "But have you given any thought at all that we're walking into a building potentially loaded with explosives?"

"They're here," Sabrina said, following her parents as they slid down into the excavation pit. "And this is their past. They lived through this. We're okay."

"Did I explain time-travel paradoxes to you?" Salem griped. "We could all get blown to bits here. Or they could live and you and I could be blown to bits."

"So this is a multiple choice question?" Before Salem could respond, still feeling excited and scared to death at the same time, Sabrina stepped off into the pit and slid down, using her feet and free hand to land upright.

The torches inside the excavated passageway flickered in the breeze flowing through, throwing yellow light and wavering shadows out onto the ground in front of the entrance.

"Allow me," Edward said, taking the lead. "After all, I'm the only one of us who is armed."

"You won't get any arguments from me," Sabrina's mom said.

146

Edward started down the passageway, one hand held back protectively to shield his future wife. His face was grim and tight. "Something's really not right here," he whispered.

Sabrina could feel it, too. A sensation of wrongness that made her skin itch. She followed her parents around the twists and turns of the passageway as it descended into the earth. An odor of decay permeated the air, making it difficult to breathe.

Edward stopped beneath a torch, peering ahead. "I thought this tunnel dead-ended."

"It does," Sabrina's mom answered.

"Not anymore. I see a room up ahead." He moved forward again.

Around the next bend, Sabrina saw the room as well. Someone *had* opened the tomb, using brute force to knock open the wall that had dead-ended the passageway. Sand and rock had spilled into the room. She crept forward, following her parents. *If I make it back to Westbridge, I'm going to have a great paper to write.*

The room was big, twenty feet square at least. Two torches hung on opposite walls, creating a pool of carbon against the limestone ceiling. The sarcophagus was on the left, the top half lying over on its side.

Subeih stood in front of the sarcophagus with a rifle aimed at them. Anger darkened his features. "I told you that creature walks among us. Look!"

Drawn by the macabre nature of the whole event, Sabrina glanced into the sarcophagus, expecting to see a mummy. However, the sarcophagus *was* empty. Only sand and broken pieces of pottery remained inside. And there was a really big bundle of dynamite sticks in the corner.

"Rameses the Great ordered Menkhotep destroyed," the bandit chief said. "She learned an evil magic that allowed her to take the youth from a man."

"She?" Sabrina asked, confused. "I thought Menkhotep was a guy."

"That was one of the things Dr. Dodge was trying to prove," her mom said. "The translations he did sometimes changed the pronoun from *he* to *she*. The professor thought Menkhotep disguised herself as a man to serve in the military, then used her friendship with Rameses I to rise in favor in the courts."

"And so it was," Subeih agreed. "But she studied her evil magicks as well. At first Menkhotep was careful about using her power, only stripping a few years from her victims to use in her spells. But in time, she grew greedy and drained nearly all of a man's life from him. My forefathers were charged with her execution, and braved her curse. But even they could not put her to rest."

"How long has she been free?" Edward asked.

"Years," the bandit chief replied. "Our stories tell of a time more than sixty years ago when one among us had his youth taken from him. It was at the time when the boy-king's tomb was found."

"Tutankhamen," Sabrina's mom whispered. "Howard Carter located the tomb in 1922. It set off an invasion of tomb raiders and Egyptologists."

"Yes," Subeih said. "Someone must have found this place then, only Menkhotep killed that person before anyone else could be told."

"But your people didn't know the location of the tomb?" Sabrina said.

"No. Otherwise we would have destroyed it long before now."

"Why?" Sabrina asked.

Her mother surveyed the hieroglyphics on the walls. "Because she has things stored here." She dragged her fingers across the engravings. "I can't make all of this out, but it says that the powerful objects Menkhotep constructed were locked in here with her body, to be forever lost from the sight of men."

"And they were," a melodic voice stated. "Even from me. For a time. When I first made my escape, I was too weak to attempt to reclaim my missing talismans. I staggered from here, dazed by the long years I had lain near death. When I grew stronger and became truly whole again months later, I realized I didn't know where my tomb lay. I'd forgotten, or maybe I'd never known. That's why Dr. Dodge's research was so important to me. He could help me find those things that I had lost that would make me even more powerful."

Sabrina turned, spotting Cantara Wasef entering the passageway. The woman still looked elegant, but her eyes glittered with dark cruelty.

"Rameses the Great considered dividing my constructions up," Cantara went on, gazing around the room. "But ultimately he decided that there was too much danger in that. He feared that someone might locate one of the pieces and track down the others as well. He hoped that they would all be lost together."

"You are Menkhotep?" Edward asked.

Sabrina was proud of the way her father handled everything so coolly. She hadn't been a witch long, but she knew that ancient evils were sometimes the most powerful.

"Yes," the woman replied. "I am Menkhotep. And I should have been a rightful ruler of this place. If Thebes had been under my control all those years ago, it would never have fallen." She looked at Sabrina's father. "Do you like my face, Edward? Am I not pretty?"

"All I see is a greedy, selfish creature," Sabrina's dad said.

Menkhotep laughed, and the sound of it scratched at the walls. "That's not what you've seen before."

"Maybe that's because he's getting a better look now," Sabrina's mom said in a hard voice.

Subeih moved without warning, lifting his rifle to his shoulder and firing. The harsh crack filled the room.

Menkhotep's hand darted forward, almost too quickly for the eye to see. She closed it and jerked her fist back. When she opened her hand again, she held the rifle bullet in her hand. "You can't hurt me. No gun or knife can ever touch me again." But she looked ten years older, fine crow's feet starting to form around her eyes.

"What about explosives, conjurer?" Subeih roared. "Have you enough lives for that as well?" He struck a match and held it to the twisted fuses of the dynamite bundle. They flared and spat burning embers.

Chapter 15

Oh, this is definitely not good, Sabrina thought as she watched the fuses swiftly incinerate.

Menkhotep gestured. In response, a dust devil rose up from the floor and swirled sand in glittering arcs. It swept over the dynamite and extinguished the fuses.

With a growl of rage, Subeih launched himself at the woman, his sword raised. She slapped the bandit chief aside easily. Subeih flew through the air and smashed against the far wall. He lay in a crumpled, unconscious heap.

Sabrina stared at the woman. *Maybe I should have stuck with the report on Mr. Kraft.*

Wrinkles ravaged Menkhotep's face, robbing her of some of her beauty. Her body suddenly looked emaciated, and her spine started to bend. Gray streaked her hair. She held a gnarled palm out to

Sabrina's dad. "Working my spells takes a lot out of me these days. Tell me, do you still find me as attractive as you once did, Edward?"

He smiled coldly at her. "I never found you attractive. Not on the inside. I like a woman with a good heart."

Menkhotep drew her hand back, and Sabrina noticed it looked more like a hard-taloned claw now. "Perhaps, then, I'll let you have hers when I've drained her body of its last few years."

"I won't let you touch her."

"You," Menkhotep stated, "won't have a choice." She started forward.

"No!" Sabrina yelped, starting forward.

Her dad stepped in front of her mom, catching the old crone's hands. "Stay back."

Menkhotep thrust her withered face into Edward's. "Grow old then, fool." A bright blue electrical current passed between them, highlighting both their bodies.

Sabrina could hardly breathe when the stench of ozone filled the room. She was certain her father was about to become a senior citizen right before her eyes in spite of his immortality.

"No!" Menkhotep pushed Edward back, her face a mask of rage and terror. "What are you?"

"Something far more human than you ever were," Edward said, taking a step forward.

Menkhotep raised her hand again. This time a violet lightning bolt flashed from her palm and struck Edward, lifting him off his feet and driving him backward. He groaned in pain when he smashed up against the wall.

But the toll on Menkhotep left her withered and mummified looking, hunched so much as to take almost a foot off her height. She started for Sabrina's mom again, but Edward pointed and the mummy rocked back on her feet, screaming as if she was mortally wounded.

Without warning, Menkhotep turned and staggered toward the center of the room. Sabrina stepped back, shocked by the age that showed in the ravaged face. The mummy stomped on the floor deliberately three times, then a section slid aside, revealing a passageway beneath.

"Don't let her go there," Edward croaked, trying to get to his feet.

"Stop," Sabrina ordered, pointing. Sparkles flashed from her forefinger and burst into green flames against the mummy's flesh. Still, Menkhotep pushed against her magic, striving to get into the opening. She hunched down and fell over the edge, dropping into the blackness below.

Sabrina's mom moved first, crossing the floor and starting down the ladder built into the wall of the passageway going down.

"Are you okay?" Sabrina asked her dad.

"Yes," he gasped, "but if that thing isn't stopped, it's only going to get more powerful." He struggled to get up.

Worried about her mom, Sabrina crossed the room and climbed down the ladder as well. The

tunnel below wasn't lighted, filled with pitch blackness. A moment later and a flashlight was switched
on, filling the narrow tunnel with pale illumination.

Sabrina pointed up a flashlight of her own as she
dropped down beside her mom. She switched it on,
then plunged after her mom, following the only
path open to them.

Their breathing rasped in the narrow confines of
the passage, and the taste of dust coated Sabrina's
mouth. She ran hard, wondering how it was her mom
could be brave enough to run after the mummy even
though she had no weapons, no magic to protect her.

The passageway ended suddenly in another room.

"Where did she go?" Sabrina's mom moved her
flashlight beam around the room. Several small crates
filled the room, but there was no sign of the mummy.
She crossed the room and started pressing against the
wall. "Is there another hidden passageway?"

A sudden rustle of clothing above Sabrina was the
only warning the teenage witch got. Then a falling
body dropped onto her, driving her to the floor.

Dazed, Sabrina gazed up as hard talons gripped
her face. She tried to reach her flashlight lying only
inches from her fingers. The beam was still strong
enough to fill the room with soft illumination.

"So, child," Menkhotep said in a raspy voice,
"have you enjoyed your youth and beauty? Because
it's yours no more." Blue fire sparked from the
glassy eyes in deepset sockets. The mummy's face
looked like a skull covered by a thin coat of leath-
ery skin.

Sabrina's mom tried to hit the mummy with her flashlight, but Menkhotep knocked her away. Grabbing the sticklike arm holding her face, the teenage witch tried to break away. But it was no use; the mummy was just too strong.

"Menkhotep." The eerie voice filled the small room.

Startled, the mummy turned her head and looked over her shoulder.

Sabrina looked too, seeing Salem sitting there, his head regally uplifted in the dulled shine of the flashlights. His black fur gleamed with a silvery-blue sheen.

"Bast," Menkhotep whispered.

"You know me," Salem said in his eerie voice. "Know also that I am the eye of Ra, the sun god and creator. You will not be allowed to succeed."

"No," the mummy said. "I have curried your favor and followed your teachings. Do not turn your face from me."

Taking advantage of Menkhotep's distraction, Sabrina yanked the mummy's hand from her face. She said,

Fighting the mummy,
That's just not fun.
Open a portal that will take it
Far from anyone.

Immediately a blue-green rectangle formed in the air behind the mummy. It opened with a flash of white-hot lightning and filled the room with the sound of roaring wind. The suction created by the gate seized the mummy, whipping her long gray hair back, then it pulled the screaming creature from Sabrina and sucked her through the portal. The portal slammed shut with the sound like two bricks being banged together. Then the portal folded itself several times and disappeared completely.

Tired and hurting, Sabrina forced herself up from the floor.

"I was beginning to think you weren't going to take the hint," Salem said.

"I was kind of busy." Sabrina glanced at her mom, who was looking at her in awe.

"Your cat talks," her mom said.

"A lot," Sabrina agreed. "It would be better if he only talked when he had something to say instead of just to hear his own voice. Or beg. He gets really obnoxious when he begs."

Her mom leaned against the wall behind her. "You'll forgive me if I take a moment here. This is a bit much."

"Sure," Sabrina said. "I think we all need one."

In the next instant her mom slumped against the wall.

"Hey," Sabrina said, starting forward. "Are you okay?"

"She's okay. She's just asleep."

Sabrina turned and watched her father step into the room.

"Menkhotep?" he asked, glancing around the

room. He moved slowly, as if at the end of his own flagging strength.

"Gone," Sabrina said. "I opened a portal and pushed her into another realm where she can't harm anyone." It was a spell she'd learned from *The Discovery of Magic* handbook when she'd been trying to create new closet space. She'd never found the clothes she'd tried to put into the other portal, but wherever Menkhotep ended up, there were also some really nice outfits.

Her father leaned against the wall. "You're not from around here."

"Not exactly."

"Where?"

"I can't tell you."

Her father nodded. "Maybe you should go back there. Things around here are going to be complicated enough to explain without trying to explain you, too. I get the feeling that if the authorities who investigate this try to look into your background, they're going to be in for some surprises."

Sabrina nodded, knowing it was true. And it was time she was getting back to her own time anyway. Enough of her questions had been answered, and staying any longer was increasing unnecessary risk. She glanced at her mom, still asleep against the wall. "Is she going to be okay?"

"I'll see to it myself."

"She's a pretty incredible lady," Sabrina said.

Her father grinned. "I'm getting that idea myself. I hope she'll find me at least half as interesting as I find her."

"She will," Sabrina said.

"Enough with the chitchat," Salem growled. "I just potentially saved the world—or at least this corner of it—from the clutches of a whacked-out mummy with delusions of grandeur."

"Assisted," Sabrina said.

"Whatever. What I'm getting at is there should be a bowl of kibble in my future somewhere about now." The cat gazed up at Sabrina with glowing yellow eyes.

"Right." Sabrina used the time-travel spell again, and a portal opened up that looked into her own bedroom. She peeked cautiously. Everything looked the same.

Even her two aunts, who were dressed in their robes and looking into her mirror with irritation. "Sabrina," Zelda said, "you've got a lot of explaining to do."

Evidently her time-travel spell hadn't exactly worked out perfectly. "Well," she said to her dad, "doom and grounding calls. Gotta go."

Edward stepped toward the portal, trying to get a better look at her aunts.

Suddenly realizing that he might recognize his sister, Sabrina grabbed Salem into her arms and dived through the portal. She landed with a thud on her bedroom floor.

When she glanced back at the mirror again, she caught a brief glimpse of her mom and dad in the mummy's tomb, then in the next instant the mirror was just a mirror again.

"I hope you've got a good explanation for how

you got into the mirror and where you've been," Hilda warned.

Sabrina thought quickly, then smiled tentatively. "I was sleepwalking?"

Excellent paper and presentation. A+.

Sabrina read the grade again, taking pride in the work she'd done. Her aunts had been pretty upset with Sabrina over the time-jaunt, but in the end they'd been more understanding than she'd had any right to expect.

"Gotta tell you, Sab, your story about your mom really rocked."

Turning around, Sabrina found Harvey standing near her locker. She hadn't even heard him come up. "I wasn't admiring the grade," she told him, feeling a little embarrassed. "I was just thinking about my mom."

"She's got a cool job," Harvey said. "I told you that. Maybe it's not quite Indiana Jones, but it's cool all the same."

She'd done the paper based on what she'd found out about her mom, weaving in bits and pieces of other stories the journals had contained. But Sabrina hadn't gone into detail regarding the tomb of Menkhotep. The official story she'd found out from researching a news archive was that the tomb was found already looted and the mummy missing. Evidently her dad had taken care of the details himself, closing down the story before it had a chance to grow.

"Yeah," Sabrina said. "You're right." She carefully folded the paper and put it inside a notebook.

"I can't believe you didn't realize that."

Sabrina shrugged. "I guess it just goes to show how you kind of take people for granted. I always just looked at her as mom, until I got to know her better. It's strange how you can be around some people all your life and never really know them."

"I guess sometimes you just gotta look at them a little different," Harvey said.

Sabrina closed her locker and they started walking down the hall together. "So, do you think you know me?"

He grinned cautiously. "Is this a trick question?"

"No."

"Okay, then no, I don't."

Sabrina felt a little hurt, then realized she'd had no business asking such a serious question so frivolously. But some of her hurt must have shown on her face because Harvey hurried on.

"You've got things and ways about you that I don't quite understand," he said. "I like the parts I've gotten to know. A lot. But I'm glad I'm still getting to know you. I enjoy that part."

"Harvey Kinkle, you say the nicest things."

Harvey shrugged. "I just say what's on my mind. Sometimes I guess I get lucky."

Sabrina couldn't help smiling. "Me, too."

About the Author

MEL ODOM lives in Moore, Oklahoma, with his wife and five children. He's the author of three other *Sabrina, the Teenage Witch* books and has also written books for *Buffy the Vampire Slayer*. He coaches basketball, baseball and football and loves watching his kids play sports. When not at a game or writing, he's known to hang out on the Internet until way after the cows come home. he can be reached at denimbyte@aol.com.

Gaze into the future and see what wonders lie in store for
Sabrina, The Teenage Witch

#32 Reality Check

Now that Sabrina is a fully licensed witch, she is allowed
to compete in the Other Realm spelling bee. She wins, and
collects first prize . . . a reality check. It may be cashed at
any time to change one instance of reality with no dire
consequences or repercussions. But how should she use it?

Aunt Hilda and Aunt Zelda are under a twenty-four-hour
time-release spell, which is causing disruption in their lives.
Harvey must pay for repairs to his car after an accident,
Libby twists her ankle before the county cheerleading
competition, and Val resigns as school newspaper editor.
Sabrina can change just one of these events . . . but
which one?

Don't miss out on any of Sabrina's magical antics — conjure up
a book from the past for a truly spellbinding read . . .

#30 Switcheroo

When Sabrina accidentally casts a powerful switcheroo
spell, she and Libby swap lives. Not only is the teenage
witch cheerleading and listening to gossip . . . she's
beginning to enjoy it! She spends less and less time with
Harvey and Valerie and more time as a social butterfly.

Eventually, Sabrina realizes she wants her old life back.
But according to Aunt Zelda and Aunt Hilda, it's not that
easy to reverse the spell. Can Sabrina pull it off? Or is she
doomed to live the rest of her life in Libby's shoes?

Nancy Drew™

Nancy Drew — Carolyn Keene — **Runaway Bride**

Nancy Drew — Carolyn Keene — **False Pretences**

Nancy Drew — Carolyn Keene — **Out of Bounds**

Nancy Drew — Carolyn Keene — **Making Waves**

Nancy Drew — Carolyn Keene — **Illusions of Evil**

Nancy Drew — Carolyn Keene — **Flirting with Danger**

Nancy Drew — Carolyn Keene — **Fatal Attraction**

Nancy Drew — Carolyn Keene — **Till Death Do Us Part**

DROP DEAD